FRIENDS

with *Baby* &

BENEFITS

T.K. LEIGH WRITING AS
TRACY LEIGH

FRIENDS WITH BABY BENEFITS

Published by Carpe Per Diem Publishing, Inc

For a full list of all of Tracy's books, including recommended reading order, please visit her website:

www.tracyleighbooks.com

Books and reading order for her spicy billionaire romance alter ego, T.K. Leigh, can be found here:

www.tkleighauthor.com

For exclusive sales and excerpts,
sign up for Tracy Leigh's VIP list!

https://www.tracyleighbooks.com/subscribe

Or scan the code below

Some of the author's books may contain content that could be triggering for sensitive readers. For a full list of content warnings for each book and/or series, please visit her website.

https://geni.us/TKLContentWarnings

Here's to friendships…
No matter the shape, size, or color.

ONE

Finn

The sharp scent of diesel fuel and grease lingers in the air as I walk around the engine truck, running through the same routine I do after every call. Inspect. Reset. Prepare for the next one. The predictability of it soothes me. It's why I did so well in the army. Why I like this job.

You follow the steps, stay sharp, and keep people safe.

Upstairs, the low murmur of conversation drifts down from the rest of the crew, their voices blending into a steady hum. But I tune it out as I continue checking the truck, shaking my head at how Reggie, our probationary officer, left his turnout gear. Everyone else has their pants lowered onto their boots so when a call comes in, all we have to do is step into them and we're on our way.

Not Reggie. His pants are lopsided, and I'm pretty sure his boots are swapped.

He'll learn that lesson soon enough.

A pair of footsteps, light yet deliberate, breaks through the ambient noise. I look up, my eyes tracking a tall, slender brunette as she walks through the open bay doors overlooking the historic downtown area of Sycamore Falls. I can't help the smile that tugs on my lips at the sight of my best friend.

I try to push down the surge of protectiveness that fills me when I notice her hair is styled and she's wearing more eyeshadow than usual. She's also dressed in a pair of slim-fitting jeans that shows off her ass perfectly and her top reveals a bit too much cleavage for my liking. It's not even a lot. I just don't like the idea of men ogling Genevieve.

I've always felt protective of her. Of everyone, really. It's in my nature, I suppose.

But after her divorce last year, I want to do everything I can to prevent her from getting hurt again.

"Where are you off to?" I ask, leaning against the engine.

"The brewery with Claire." She lifts a covered casserole dish. "But I wanted to drop this off first."

I raise an eyebrow as the familiar aroma of tomatoes and garlic invades my senses. "Is that lasagna?"

"I was in the mood to cook."

I push off the truck, eyeing her with suspicion. "Is everything okay?"

While Genevieve is a great cook, I know her better than most people. She typically only makes lasagna when she's had a bad day and needs to feel good.

"I'm fine, Finn," she assures me. "You mentioned it was John's night to cook, so I figured I'd be a shitty friend if I didn't save you from whatever culinary catastrophe he plans to make. Consider this *my* version of saving lives."

I blow out a low chuckle. "You're definitely doing God's work by saving us from that."

"Don't I know it?" She winks. "Just don't let him reheat this lasagna. He'll probably ruin it."

"I'll take care of it myself," I assure her, taking the casserole dish from her. "Want to come up for a minute? That way, the guys can personally thank the woman who saved their lives."

A gentle laugh falls from her throat. "Sure."

The faint click of her heels on the metal steps mixes with the distant sound of a news anchor on the TV in the lounge as she trails behind me.

At the top of the stairs, I pause and face her. "Wait here a sec."

"Of course."

By this point, she knows the drill. While we're used to getting visitors, the fire department is mostly men. Some days, it can be a bit like a fraternity house, minus the keg parties.

I push through the door into the lounge, where Murphy is sprawled on the couch, John is raiding the fridge, and Reggie is flipping through channels like it's an Olympic sport. Cappy is in his office just off the lounge, probably filling out paperwork after the last call.

"What's that?" Murphy asks as I head toward the kitchen area and set the casserole tray onto the counter before turning on the oven.

"Genevieve made lasagna."

Murphy holds his hands together and looks at the ceiling. "Thank you, Lord, for sparing my life tonight."

John shoots him a glare as he closes the refrigerator door. "You're an asshole."

"And you're a horrible cook."

"Genevieve's coming in, so try to act somewhat civilized," I warn them.

Murphy sits up, looking wounded. "We're civilized."

"You're just one step ahead of a Neanderthal on the evolutionary chart," I say, then shoot my attention over to Reggie. "And go fix your turnout gear, probie. It's a fucking catastrophe. Do you need me to mark your left and right shoe like a goddamn preschooler?"

"It's not that bad."

"Go fix it, probie," Cappy calls out from his office. "The twenty extra seconds it will take for you to get your shit on can be the difference between life and death."

"Yes, sir," he mumbles, pulling himself off the couch as I open the door for Genevieve.

It doesn't escape my notice the way Reggie looks at her as he passes.

I don't like it.

"Gen!" Murphy jumps to his feet and approaches her, enveloping her in a tight hug. "You're a saint. Thank you for saving my life tonight."

John groans. "I mess up one tuna noodle casserole, and suddenly I'm the worst cook in the state."

"One?" Murphy snorts, releasing Genevieve and facing him. "What about the chicken Alfredo incident?"

"I thought the sauce would cook faster if I increased the temperature."

"And the pot roast?" I add, opening the oven and setting the casserole dish inside.

John glares at me. "The oven was acting weird."

From his office, Cappy's voice booms, "Don't forget the time he turned chili night into a training exercise."

John throws his hands up in surrender. "Fine. Maybe I need some help in the kitchen. Happy?"

"Very," Murphy says with a satisfied smirk.

Genevieve just shakes her head, her smile soft and genuine. "Well, I'm glad I could help."

"Want to stay and eat?" I ask her.

"I can't. Claire's probably already waiting for me."

"Did you have dinner?"

"I had some pasta."

"Will you text me when you get home so I know you're okay?"

She rolls her eyes, feigning annoyance, but eventually treats me to her usual heartwarming smile. "Of course." She shifts her attention past me. "Have a good night, boys."

"Thanks, Gen," they all chime in.

She looks back my way for a beat before turning and heading out of the lounge, her heels echoing as she continues down the stairs.

As soon as her retreating footsteps are no longer audible, Murphy turns to me with a sly grin. "When are you finally going to make your move?"

"What are you talking about?" I reply, heading back to the oven to check on the lasagna.

It was still relatively warm when Genevieve brought it over, so it shouldn't take too long to reheat.

"You and Gen. You'd be good together. Anyone with two eyes can see it."

"Yeah, man," Reggie says as he re-enters the lounge. "I've only been here a few months and even *I* can see it."

"Shut up, probie," I retort. "This is a grown-up conversation."

He shakes his head, but doesn't argue back. He

can't. Not until he's out of his probationary period. Until then, he's low man on the totem pole and has to pay his dues. Just like we all did.

But even though I can give Reggie shit, I can't do the same to Murphy. He has the most seniority out of all of us, except for Cappy. And when he pins me with a glare, I know he doesn't plan on dropping this conversation. Not yet anyway.

"She's my best friend," I repeat the same argument I give to everyone who questions my relationship with Genevieve.

Murphy isn't the first person to bring up the possibility of crossing that line with her, especially now that she's divorced. I've fielded these types of questions for as long as I can remember. No one thinks men and women can just be friends without sex eventually entering into the equation.

I value our friendship too much to do anything to put it at risk.

"We've known each other since we were in preschool," I remind Murphy. "She's like a…sister."

John raises an eyebrow. "I could be wrong, but most people don't eye-fuck their sisters the way you just eye-fucked Gen."

"I didn't just eye-fuck her," I retort, grabbing a bottle of water from the fridge, although he's probably right.

I *am* a guy, after all. And Genevieve Thomas is absolutely beautiful. From her long legs to her full lips and everything in between. You'd have to be blind not to be attracted to her.

There was a time when I *did* look at Genevieve like she was just a sister. Or, more appropriately, a gender-neutral sibling. I knew she was a girl, but she didn't feel like a girl to me. For one, she'd play video games with me. We'd collect worms together for our pet worm collection, much to my mother's horror. Hell, we even had farting competitions.

That all changed the summer before our freshman year of high school.

I'll never forget that first warm day when I invited her over my parents' house to go for a swim and I saw her in her bathing suit.

It wasn't the first time we'd swam together.

But it was the first time I realized she had boobs.

I'm not too proud to admit I told her I needed to go to the bathroom, where I proceeded to jerk off as I looked out the window at her in her bikini.

So no. As much as I like to tell everyone I've never looked at her as anything more than a sister, that's not entirely true.

Regardless, she's too important to me to let my hormones get in the way.

"Fine." Murphy leans back in his chair, grinning. "If you're not interested, maybe I'll ask her out."

"She's going through a divorce, asshole."

"Hasn't her divorce been finalized for close to a year?"

I shrug dismissively, officially hating this conversation.

"I think that's long enough to wait. Don't you?" he taunts with a waggle of his brow.

"Ask her out if you really want," I say nonchalantly, knowing the more I resist, the more he'll read into my reluctance. "Don't be disappointed when she turns you down."

It doesn't matter I know Murphy has no intention of actually asking her out. Just the thought of her on a date with someone sends a surge of something hot and ugly through my chest.

I tell myself it's just because I don't want her to get hurt again so soon after her divorce. That's the only possible explanation for the way my body reacts to the idea of her dating someone.

I refuse to consider the alternative.

Not when she's a friend.

Only a friend.

TWO

Genevieve

The brewery is bustling tonight with the sort of energy that can only be found on a Friday night in a small town. Every corner hums with laughter and conversation as a mixture of locals and tourists celebrate the end of another week.

There was a time when this town was the last place I'd want to be, especially after Ethan told me he'd fallen out of love with me and wanted a divorce. I hated the idea of returning to the place where I grew up, only for everyone in this small town to talk about my failed marriage behind my back.

All it took was a few days of being back here to realize this was exactly what I needed. I now have a job I love as the head librarian instead of working in an administrative position for the library system in

San Francisco. I was even able to afford the down payment on a charming cottage a few miles away from downtown. I have everything I've always wanted.

Well, *almost* everything. There's one thing that's still missing.

I fear it always will be now.

"All right, spill," my sister's voice cuts through the sound of a classic rock song playing over the speakers.

I dart my eyes back to Claire and furrow my brow as I take a sip of my IPA. "Spill what?"

"You seem off today. What's up?"

I should have known she'd pick up on that. If anyone could see through my forced smile, it's my sister.

And Finn.

"It's nothing," I exhale, not sure if I'm ready for this conversation, especially in a noisy bar where anyone can overhear.

News travels fast in a small town, and people love a juicy story. No doubt, this would be front-page news tomorrow if word got out.

"You're a terrible liar," she snips back, raising her beer to her lips. "Come on, Gen. Just tell me. You know I'll eventually get it out of you."

I take a long sip of my own beer, fully aware she's right. Claire's like a bloodhound when she's onto something. She'll sniff out the truth, whether I'm ready to share or not.

"I've been thinking about…having a baby," I announce.

My sister's mouth falls open, and for a second, she just stares at me. Whatever she expected me to say, it definitely wasn't this.

"A baby? As in your *own* baby?"

"Yes," I respond, my voice soft but firm.

She blinks, then leans back in her chair. "Wow. Okay. I mean, it's not that crazy, since you've always wanted a family."

"I don't know if it's actually in the cards for me," I admit.

"Because of…everything?" She waves her hand around, avoiding any mention of my recent divorce.

"No." I quickly shake my head. "I've started looking into the process of artificial insemination. While insurance will cover the procedure once I meet my ridiculously high deductible, it won't cover the donor sperm. That alone is about two grand per vial."

"Two thousand dollars for sperm?" she shoots back in disbelief, her eyes wide.

"On average, yes."

"Damn." She brings her glass back to her lips.

"And because the success rate for IUI isn't that great, I could be spending all that money for nothing."

"Can't you just do IVF?" Claire smooths a dark wave behind her ear. "Isn't the success rate for that higher?"

"It is. But because my doctor didn't find any signs of fertility problems, my insurance company won't pay for IVF unless I do six rounds of IUI first. Even after that, they'll only cover half. Essentially, to be eligible for IVF, I'd have to potentially pay upwards of fifteen grand first. Possibly more. I've looked into adoption, but being single doesn't help. The legal fees alone would wipe out my savings." I push out a long sigh as I swipe the condensation off my pint glass. "I guess I'm just suffering from a bit of sticker shock."

Claire takes another sip of her beer, the amber liquid reflecting the dim bar lights. "What if you just do it the old-fashioned way?"

"The old-fashioned way?"

"Yeah. You know. Sex."

"Thanks for the clarification. I know how these things work."

"Right. So if you want a baby, just get knocked up. No need to spend all that money."

"There's just one problem."

She scrunches her nose. "What's that?"

"I'm single, remember?"

"So?" She shrugs like it's no big deal. "Find a guy with traits you like, explain what you're looking for, and ask him to help you out. No strings attached. He gets to have some fun with an awesome girl, and you get a baby. No need to involve the insurance company."

I laugh nervously. "That's insane."

"It's practical," she counters, her green eyes bright with conviction. "I recently read an article about the rise in pre-natal agreements."

"Pre-natal agreements? What's that? Like some sort of…contract?"

"It's not legally binding, but it can be used as evidence if there's ever a dispute. It's for situations where two people conceive a child on purpose, but they're not romantically involved. More and more women are looking into having a baby on their own without the complications of a committed relationship. These agreements set out expectations up front."

"It would be simpler in theory," I admit. "And cheaper."

"Exactly," Claire says, her voice triumphant. "You have a good job, your own house. Plus, you were raised by a kick-ass single mom yourself who taught us we don't need a man to do anything we want. You can totally do this on your own. But you won't have to, since you know Mom and I will help you anytime you need it." She squeals. "I can't wait to be the cool aunt."

"You'll be the *only* aunt," I remind her, trying not to get my hopes up for something that may never happen.

"Even if I weren't, I'd still be the cool aunt."

"You certainly would." I give her a sincere smile, then relax into my chair, contemplating her suggestion.

"So what do you think?"

"It could be the beer," I begin with a small laugh, "but I guess it wouldn't hurt to make a list."

Claire grins and pulls a notepad from her purse.

"It doesn't mean I'm on board," I add quickly. "Just that I'm…exploring my options."

"Now you're talking." She flips to a blank page. "What traits are you looking for?"

"Healthy," I answer without hesitation. "It probably sounds shallow, but I'd prefer someone with decent genes."

She makes a note in her notebook before returning her gaze to me. "What else?"

"Intelligent. Someone who understands irregardless isn't a real word."

Claire laughs under her breath. "Only you would have grammar requirements for a sperm donor."

I shrug, sipping on my beer. "I can't stand that word. It's like nails on a chalkboard." A shiver rolls through me at the mere thought.

"Anything else?" she probes.

I bite my lower lip and rack my brain. I've looked at potential donors in sperm banks, but it all seemed so overwhelming. This does, too.

Thankfully, the beer helps.

"Compassionate. Kind. Gentle. I may not be raising the kid with this person, but I'd prefer him to not be a complete asshole. After all, I *am* going to have to sleep with whomever it is to get pregnant."

"True." She makes a few more notes, then looks up. "Now who should the lucky guy be?" She scans the bar, tapping her pen against her mouth. "What about Mike Stevens? He's easy on the eyes."

I follow her line of sight and survey Mike's muscular frame as he stands against the bar with a few guys he works with.

"Plus, he does construction, so he'll probably be good with his hands, if you know what I mean."

"I'm not interested in whether he'll be good with his hands. Only what kind of DNA he'll impart to my kid."

"Should we put him on your list of potential candidates?"

"I don't know." I sigh. "All he talked about back in high school was how many hours he spent in the gym that week. While it's obvious he's committed to his health, it's a little…much."

"Okay. More brains than brawn."

We return our attention to the bustling taproom, scrutinizing the men we've known all our lives. Which is turning out to be more of a hinderance than anything. Because we know who had horrible acne as a teenager. Who picked their nose. Whose locker reeked every time we walked by.

"What about Josh Taylor?" Claire suggests after a few minutes. "He's a lawyer. Plus, he's also recently divorced. He has two kids so you know he can get the job done."

I pinch my lips together as I try to imagine what our baby would look like. He's not a bad-looking guy, but I'm not overly enthusiastic about the prospect of his DNA. I can't quite put my finger on why.

"It's a possibility," I finally say.

Claire's eyes light up as she quickly jots down his name on the sheet of paper before returning her attention to the growing crowd.

"How about Carter Wilson? Tall, good-looking, and he has a steady job."

"True, but he doesn't read," I tell her. "When I ran into him after I first moved back and told him I was the new head librarian, he looked confused, then asked why people would read when there was television and social media. I'd rather not pass those genes onto my child."

"Duly noted."

As we're mid-debate over whether Jake Hamilton's dimples outweigh his strange laugh, a siren sounds and a bright red fire engine drives past the floor-to-ceiling windows of the brewery.

Claire's eyes widen, and she darts her gaze toward me.

"Oh, no," I retort immediately, sensing the wheels spinning in her head. "Don't even think about it."

"Why not?" she asks innocently. "He checks all the boxes. Tall, good-looking, athletic, smart, and he likes to read. Plus, he's a firefighter." A visible shiver rolls through her. "That's pretty damn sexy."

"Why don't you ask him out then?" I swallow a long gulp of my beer, pushing down the jealousy bubbling inside me over the mere thought, even if I know Claire would never do that.

She narrows her gaze on me. "You have to admit it's a good idea."

"No, it's not," I say firmly.

"Why?"

"Because Finn's my best friend."

"All the more reason it's a good idea. If you're going to do this, it should be with someone you trust. Someone you know will honor your wishes. We both know Finn would do anything for you. I have no doubt he'd do this for you if you asked."

I bring my beer up to my lips and sip it. I can't argue with Claire. Finn probably *would* agree if I asked this of him. But can I really do that? Can I really cross that line?

"Plus, the sex would most likely be incredible. God doesn't gift a man with that incredible body and make him horrible in bed. You can't sit there and tell me you've never wondered what it'd be like."

Of course I've thought about it. Probably more than I should have. But I'll never admit it. Finn has always been one of the few people in my life I can depend on.

I can't complicate things with him.

Asking him to get me pregnant?

That would most definitely complicate things.

"Finn's a friend," I declare. "Nothing more."

She studies me for several protracted moments, then exhales, scanning the bar once more. I do the same, but my thoughts are no longer consumed with finding someone with adequate DNA.

Now all I can think about is Finn.

THREE

Genevieve

The document blurs on my computer screen, the letters swirling in front of me. I blink a few times, trying to refocus, but it's no use. Instead of working on a proposal for a new class aimed at teaching older adults computer skills, I keep replaying my conversation with Claire.

As crazy as it may sound on the surface, trying to conceive naturally first has some merit. But can I ask someone to get me pregnant, then give up all rights to their child? Maybe I should just suck it up and fork over the money for donor sperm instead. It would be less complicated, even if infinitely more expensive with less than stellar results.

God, I hate this. Why does this have to be so difficult? And expensive? I bet if men were the ones who could get pregnant, there wouldn't be this many barriers. At the very least, it would be infinitely more affordable.

A soft knock startles me, and I snap my head up as Finn steps in, holding two paper cups.

"Coffee delivery," he announces, closing the door with his foot.

He looks so casual in a pair of cargo shorts and a black t-shirt that clings to his chest and biceps, displaying his muscular physique. He wears the same smile that usually puts me at ease.

Except today.

Right now, the sight of him only reminds me of my conversation with Claire, causing my pulse to race for a reason I don't want to begin to examine, especially after her suggestion that I add his name to the list.

At the reminder, I suck in a quick breath, remembering the list is currently in plain view on the corner of my desk. I try to grab it without drawing his attention, but Finn's sharp eyes catch me before I can.

"What's that?" He quirks an eyebrow, setting my coffee down on my desk and sitting across from me.

"Nothing," I say quickly.

Too quickly.

He tilts his head, his mouth quirking into a half-smile that says he doesn't believe me.

"If it's nothing, why are you acting like you just

got caught stealing office supplies?" He takes a sip of coffee.

I glance at the paper in my hand, then back at him, hesitating. There's no point in keeping this from him. It's not like I'll be able to hide my pregnancy. I wouldn't want to anyway. He's my best friend. I'll need his support.

"It's a list," I finally announce.

"Of?"

"Potential candidates."

His brow furrows. "Candidates for what?"

"For their DNA."

"Their…DNA?"

"I want to have a baby. With the cost of both IUI and IVF being what they are, I'm toying with the idea of trying to get pregnant naturally first."

He spits out his coffee, his eyes widening as he stares at me like I've sprouted another head. "You mean…sex?"

My pulse kicks up in response to hearing him say that word in his deep voice. It shouldn't affect me like it does, but it makes me wonder what his bedroom voice might sound like. What kind of depraved fantasies he'd whisper in my ear.

I quickly push down the thought, hoping he can't pick up on the fact that my skin is on fire. Finn's never shown a modicum of interest in me. I'm perfectly okay with that. His friendship is too important.

Hell, after my divorce, his friendship is *everything*.

"That's usually how these things work." I set the list back on my desk and tuck a loose strand of dark hair behind my ear, looking anywhere but directly into Finn's blue eyes. "Considering I'm in my thirties and divorced, I don't have time to wait around for Mr. Right before my chances of conceiving drastically reduce. Honestly, I'm not even interested in a relationship. I don't need a husband to have a baby. I just need some decent sperm."

"That's all you want? To get knocked up and for the guy to disappear?"

"Exactly. I could try IUI, but I have a pretty high deductible on my insurance. Even if I didn't, they'll only cover the procedure, not the sperm. Plus, the chances of conception aren't much better than trying naturally, so Claire suggested trying that first to save some money."

"How much money are we talking about?" He rests his leg on his opposite thigh, genuinely curious.

"A single vial of sperm costs about two grand, and they recommend buying three once you find a donor you prefer."

Finn coughs on his coffee yet again. "Two grand for sperm?" He looks into the distance. "Maybe I should look into donating. Getting paid for jerking off? Sounds like a win-win to me."

He flashes me a charismatic smile before shifting his gaze to the paper on my desk.

"Are these guys aware they're in the running?"

"No. And they're not 'in the running.' We were just…brainstorming possibilities."

"May I?" He nods at the sheet of paper.

I hesitate, not immediately handing it over, but eventually do, the seconds seeming to stretch as he rakes his gaze down it.

"You really think Mitchell Brighton would make a good dad? He likes pineapple on his pizza."

I roll my eyes, yanking the paper from him. "That's not exactly an inherited trait. Plus, I'm not looking for someone who will be a good dad. In fact, I'm looking for someone who *doesn't* want the responsibility. Mitchell is notoriously anti-relationship."

Finn snatches the list back from me. "Thomas Hubert? Seriously?"

"He's a good guy. An investment banker so he's smart."

"I'm pretty sure he irons his jeans. I've never seen a single wrinkle on his clothes. Or his face. He probably shaves five times a day."

I shake my head, although he has a point. Thomas is always extremely put together. I like order in my life, but Thomas seems to take it to the extreme.

"What about Murphy? He's on the list. You two are close."

Finn's jaw tightens for a second before he covers it with a smirk. "Other than the fact that if he did something to upset you I'd have to kill him, the guy spent last summer posting videos of himself doing viral dances. Is that really the legacy you want to pass on to your child?"

"Dancing isn't a genetic trait, either," I counter.

"You haven't seen him dance. If I were you, I wouldn't take the risk."

I push out an exasperated sigh. "Why do I get the feeling you'll find something wrong with everyone on this list?"

"Because no one's good enough for you, Genevieve," he says in a soft voice, his light tone shifting to one of sincerity. "Nothing you do or say will ever convince me otherwise."

I part my lips to respond, but no words come. Instead, as our eyes meet and I see the kindness within, all I can think about is Claire's suggestion to ask Finn. That if there's anyone I can trust with this, it's the man sitting across from me.

"But in all seriousness," he says, clearing his throat. "I know how much you've always wanted a child. If this is what you need to make that happen, I support you." He reaches across the desk and covers my hand with his, giving it a gentle squeeze. "Whatever you need, I'm here for you."

I give him a tight smile. "Thanks, Finn."

He holds my gaze for several more moments before pulling away and sipping on his coffee. "Oh, before I forget. I picked up a shift for Murphy on Wednesday. Do you mind swinging by to check on Duke and feed him?"

"Of course." I give him a smile, grateful for the change in conversation. "You know how much I love your dog."

"You're the best." He winks, then tells me about some call they had over the weekend, the shock of my plan to get knocked up now long forgotten.

At least by Finn.

But as I try to focus on what he's saying, my brain is consumed with the idea of what my baby would look like with his DNA.

FOUR

Finn

"Did you have a fire last night?" Jude scans my disheveled appearance as I move toward the bar in the brewery. The late afternoon sun filters through the floor-to-ceiling windows, lending a warm glow to everything in sight.

The benefit of my brother owning this place and being the head brew master is I get to drink all the free beer I want.

And I need it right now.

Jude reaches for a glass and places it under one of the taps, then sets the honey brown ale in front of me.

Nodding my thanks, I take a sip, hoping to find some clarity.

Although, I doubt anyone's ever found much clarity at the bottom of a glass of beer.

Still, I'm willing to try anything.

I've been thinking about Genevieve's list all damn week. Every time I recall the names on it, a knot forms in my chest. At first, I told myself it was just the idea of her going through something so big alone that unsettled me.

I know better.

It's not just the thought of her being alone. It's the idea of some guy who doesn't deserve her stepping up when I know I could.

When I know I *should*.

"I've been off," I tell my brother as he leans against the back counter, folding his arms over his chest.

Despite it being only a little after five on a Thursday, the taproom is packed with people hoping to taste one of the beers he's famous for. And not just in our small town, but all over the west coast and the rest of the country.

And I get to reap the benefits.

"Working a twenty-four tomorrow, though," I add when he remains silent, his blue eyes scrutinizing me.

"Then…"

"You ever feel like you're about to do something that could either be the best or dumbest thing you've ever done?"

"Every damn day," he replies with a low chuckle. "What's on your mind, Finn?"

"I'm thinking about offering to help Genevieve have a baby," I blurt out before I can stop myself.

I've been wanting to talk to someone about this since Genevieve first told me her plan. As close as I am to the other guys at the fire department, this is a bit of a personal topic, especially for Genevieve. I've always been close to my family. I just hope my brother can help me navigate the warring thoughts in my head.

After a beat of stunned silence, he says, "I'm going to need you to back up and tell me what you mean." He grabs a glass and heads to the row of taps, filling it and taking a sip, which surprises me. He normally doesn't drink while he's working.

I guess this conversation warrants an exception.

"She wants a baby, but after her divorce, she has absolutely no desire to date," I explain. "She's decided to have a baby on her own."

"So…what?" He tilts his head. "You'd provide a sample?"

"Not exactly." I tip back my glass and take several large gulps, downing half of my beer in order to steel myself for where this conversation is headed.

"But…" He furrows his brows in confusion before the realization dawns on him, his eyes going wide. "She's going for a more…natural approach."

"It's a mistake, isn't it?" I ask.

"I didn't say that. I just…" He trails off, seemingly

having difficulty wrapping his head around this bomb I just dropped. "How did this come about?"

"She's been looking into her options, but her insurance only covers certain things. And they require her to go through six rounds of IUI before they'll even consider covering IVF."

"What's IUI?"

"Intra-uterine insemination."

"Right."

"Her insurance has a high deductible she needs to meet before they'll cover anything. Even then, they'll only cover the procedure, not the donor vial. And each vial can cost about two grand."

Jude spits out his beer, his reaction similar to mine when I learned this. "Damn. Maybe I should donate sperm."

"I said the same thing." I chuckle, grateful for the break in tension, regardless of how brief. "But the chances of getting pregnant with IUI are only slightly better than going the natural route, so she'd have to spend upwards of fifteen grand just to be eligible for IVF. Then there are all the shots."

"Shots?" He arches a brow.

"Yeah. She'll have to stab her ass or thigh or something with a needle." I don't tell him how I learned all of this. That I've spent the past few days researching everything about IUI and IVF in the hopes of giving myself some direction about what to do.

It hasn't.

If anything, it's only confused me more.

"All for the chance to have a baby?" Jude remarks.

"For some people, it's the only way they *can* have a baby. But…"

"Yes?"

"She doesn't have fertility issues, so it's possible…"

"For her to conceive naturally," he finishes.

"She has a fucking list."

"A list?"

"Of potential baby daddies."

"At least you made the first cut," he offers with a smile.

"That's the thing…" I tilt back my beer and guzzle the rest of it. "I didn't." I slam my glass onto the counter, a renewed ache forming in my chest over the thought.

I shouldn't care. It shouldn't matter that my name was nowhere to be found on that list. Hell, my name *shouldn't* have been on that list.

But it stings.

"What do you mean?" He grabs my glass and refills it.

"I'm her best friend and I wasn't on the goddamn list."

"Maybe she doesn't want to do anything to ruin your friendship." He slides me a fresh beer. "If she's going to be a single mom, she'll need to lean on people for support. She'll need to lean on *you* for support."

"And I told her I'd give her all the help she needs. Changing diapers. Midnight feedings. Whatever. But to learn she's okay with taking DNA from Mitchell Brighton? Or…or fucking Thomas Hubert? I'm sorry, but I think my DNA is infinitely better. I doubt they've got the swimmers to seal the deal."

"There's no guarantee yours are any better."

"My swimmers are just fine. I had them tested."

This additional piece of information causes Jude to spit out his beer yet again, leaving him momentarily speechless.

"You're serious about this. Aren't you?" he asks softly.

I run a hand down my face. "I don't know. One minute, I'm convinced it's a horrible idea. The next, it doesn't seem so bad. We get along great. We practically live with each other as it is. She trusts me, and if she's going to try to get pregnant naturally, shouldn't trust be the most important factor? Or am I crazy for even thinking about this?"

"I don't think you're crazy. I think you're a good friend. Gen's lucky to have you."

He places a hand on my shoulder and gives it a squeeze before pulling back and leaning against the back of the bar.

"Look, I'm not going to tell you what to do here.

If you're this worked up over it, you probably already know what you want. You're just looking for someone to give you permission. There's only one person who can do that." He narrows his gaze on me. "And I'm looking at him."

FIVE

Finn

As I finish the rest of my beer, I can't stop thinking about what Jude said. How, if I'm this worked up about the situation, I already know what to do. Can I really ask Genevieve to consider me? And what would that mean for our friendship if she turns me down?

But am I willing to stand by as she goes through this with someone else?

Someone who may not honor her wishes?

Someone who might hurt her? Make things difficult for her?

I hoped talking to my brother would give me clarity. But I'm even more confused than I was before. I doubt the beer is helping. Instead of having another, I say my goodbyes and head out.

The summer air hits me as I step outside, warm and sweet. The streets of downtown Sycamore Falls are alive with people — families heading to dinner, couples strolling hand in hand, kids darting between storefronts. It's the kind of lively chaos that's supposed to feel comforting, a reminder of the summer nights I spent with my family when I was a kid.

Tonight, it just makes everything worse.

I shove my hands into my pockets and start walking with no destination in mind as I try to make sense of my thoughts.

As I walk, Genevieve's list continues to flash before my eyes, the names blurring together. Each one feels like a punch to the gut. Not because they're bad guys.

Because they're not me.

I can't shake the image of her with someone else, someone she doesn't love, just to have a baby. She deserves more than that. She deserves someone who cares about her, who knows her better than anyone else. Someone who would move heaven and earth to make sure she and that baby have everything they need.

Someone like me.

I pass by a park bench where a woman sits cradling a baby. She's rocking gently, murmuring something soft and sweet. The baby's tiny hand curls around her finger, clinging to her like she's their whole world.

The sight hits me like a sucker punch, and I stop in my tracks.

For as long as I can remember, Genevieve has wanted this. A baby. A family. All things I've never wanted for myself. Not because I'm against them, but because that desire has never burned in me the way it does in her.

But this? Helping her have a baby without all the strings? Maybe this is something I *can* do.

The knot in my chest loosens enough for me to breathe again. I don't know if this is the best idea I've ever had or the dumbest, but I know one thing for sure. I can't stand by and let someone else do this with her and not say something.

Spinning on my heels, I practically run down the sidewalk toward the municipal parking lot and hop in my truck, feeling more certain than I have in a long time.

When I pull into the driveway of Genevieve's house, I kill the ignition and grip the steering wheel, staring at the cozy white cottage with blue door, my heart thundering in my ears as adrenaline courses through my veins.

I run into burning buildings for a living. Spent four years in the army risking my life on a daily basis.

But this?

This may be the scariest thing I've ever done.

But I'll regret it if I don't.

I'm out of my truck before I can talk myself out

of it, my legs carrying me up to her front door in a way that makes me think there's some bigger force at play here.

I'm about to punch my code into her door like I normally do whenever I come over. But I don't feel right about barging in on her, then having this conversation. Instead, I press the doorbell.

The sound echoes through the house, and time slows to a crawl.

I don't hear any movement at first.

Maybe she's out with her sister.

Or worse, maybe she's already out with someone on her list, getting the ball rolling with some other guy.

The thought nearly makes me turn around.

Finally, soft footsteps shuffle inside, growing louder as they approach, each one like a drumbeat counting down to something I pray I'm ready for.

The lock turns and the door swings open, revealing Genevieve in yoga pants and a faded T-shirt that says "Try reading books instead of banning them". Her dark hair is piled in a messy bun, a few loose strands curling around her face. No makeup. No effort.

And still, she's beautiful.

She's *always* beautiful.

"Why did you ring the doorbell? Did you forget your code?"

For a split second, I consider coming up with some

other excuse for being here and letting her plan unfold without me.

But the thought has my stomach in knots.

"I didn't forget anything." My voice is rougher than I expect. "But you did."

She blinks repeatedly, a small furrow forming in her brow. "I did?"

I nod. "Your list. You forgot a name."

"I'm not sure I—"

"You forgot *my* name."

Her eyes widen as she stares at me for what feels like an eternity, my words seeming to echo in the space between us.

"Finn, I—"

"I know it's crazy," I begin, pacing the length of her porch as I tug on my hair, making me look even more disheveled than I probably already do. "But you're my best friend, Genevieve."

"And you're mine."

"Which is why I want to be the one to give this to you." I approach her, instinctively cupping her face. My thumbs brush the smooth skin of her cheekbones, and I don't miss the way her breath catches.

It's not the first time I've touched her, but something about this moment feels different. Bigger, somehow.

"Do you really want to have a baby?" I ask, my voice low. "A family?"

Her lips part, but it takes a second for her to speak. "You know I do."

"Then if this is the path you're taking, you need someone you can trust. Someone you know won't want anything more from you."

"And you'll never want anything more."

It's not a question, but a statement. Still, I can't help but hear an undercurrent of something in her words. Disappointment maybe?

I drop my hands from her, putting space between us. "Our friendship is too important to me. You can trust me to keep the lines firmly drawn."

She presses her lips together and studies me for several protracted moments. I expect for her to tell me it's a bad idea. Hell, I *know* it's a bad idea.

That's not enough of a reason for me to walk away or rescind my offer.

"You'll need you to get tested for STDs and fertility."

"Already done."

I reach into my back pocket and pull out my cell, scrolling to the email I received earlier in the day with my test results. I hold out the screen so she can see for herself.

"My pH levels are good. Sperm concentration is way over 16 million per millimeter. Motility is over 50%. According to the clinic, I can get the job done."

She releases a nervous laugh. "You've really given this some thought."

"A bit," I answer nonchalantly, although I haven't been able to think about much else since Monday.

"I… I don't know what to say. It's a lot to think about. I started that list with Claire for fun, so this…"

"You don't need to give me an answer right now. Just say you'll think about it. No matter what you decide, I'll still support you. I just… I want you to have everything you deserve and don't want you to get hurt in the process. That's all."

Something flickers in her gaze before she steps forward and wraps her arms around me. Her head rests against my chest, and I close my eyes, inhaling the familiar scent of her shampoo.

"Thanks, Finn. I'll think about it."

SIX

Genevieve

The scent of freshly brewed coffee fills the air as I sit at a small corner table in Bean & Bloom, waiting for Claire. The local café is bustling this morning, the chatter of locals and the hum of the espresso machine blending into a comforting environment. I wrap my hands around my cup, letting the warmth seep into my fingers and hopefully settle my unease after Finn's unexpected proposition.

I tossed and turned all night thinking about it. Sure, there was a part of me that had wanted him to offer to add his name to the list when he found it. But over the past few days, I convinced myself that asking someone to get me pregnant to save money was a ridiculous idea to begin with. Instead, I made a new list — one of anonymous donors from a sperm bank my doctor recommended.

Which is what I was doing last night when Finn showed up and asked me to add his name to my original list.

I shouldn't even be considering it. I should just tell him I've changed my mind and am going to use an anonymous donor instead.

But there's another part of me that thinks it wouldn't hurt to try this way first, especially since Finn's offering, eliminating the prospect of having to proposition someone to knock me up. Not to mention the amount of money I'd save.

The bell over the door jingles, and I glance up, hoping it's Claire.

Instead, Finn's mom, Danielle, steps inside, holding Finn's nephew, Jeremiah, on her hip. My heart lifts at the sight of them.

Danielle has always been like a second mother to me, and little Jeremiah is about the cutest kid I've ever seen. Of course he is. He has those Lawrence genes — dazzling smile, full head of dark hair, and those signature dimples every single one of the Lawrence brothers has. For a split second, I imagine what Finn's baby would look like. What *our* baby would look like.

I quickly push down the thought when Danielle spots me, her face lighting up with a smile as she makes her way toward me. "Genevieve, sweetheart. How are you?"

"I'm doing well." I stand to give her a quick hug before turning my attention to Jeremiah. "And how's this little guy?"

"Oh, you know. Keeping me on my toes," Danielle replies with a laugh. "But I love every second of spending time with him, despite the circumstances."

I nod, all too familiar with the reason Danielle now spends every second she's not working at the local salon taking care of her grandkids.

Her oldest son, Hayden, lost his wife tragically in a car accident late last year. Instead of staying in Chicago, he decided to move home to be closer to family. While Jeremiah has adjusted to the change fairly well, his older sister, Presley, hasn't. She hasn't spoken since her mother died.

Danielle sets Jeremiah down, and he toddles over to me, his arms outstretched.

I crouch to scoop him up, letting him babble in his toddler language while I make exaggerated nods and gasps as if I understand every word.

"Do you mind watching him for a minute so I can get a coffee?"

"Of course. I've got him."

"Thanks."

I give her a smile, then turn my attention back to Jeremiah, who seems enthralled by my necklace. He grabs it in his chubby hand and says, "Gigi, shiny."

"Yes." I chuckle. "Gigi likes shiny things."

"Well, that was fast," Claire's voice cuts through.

I look up as she approaches the table.

"A week ago, we came up with a plan for you to have a baby, and now you have one."

I roll my eyes. "I'm watching him so Danielle can grab a coffee." I push one of the coffee cups across the table toward Claire as she sits.

"I can see it now," she announces after taking a sip of her drink.

"See what?"

"You as a mom. I couldn't before. Now I can."

I smile at Jeremiah as he continues to examine my necklace with the scrutiny of an investigator. "I want a family. Why shouldn't I have a baby just because I'm not married?"

"Damn straight. Fuck the patriarchy," Claire retorts.

"Watch your language." I shoot my younger sister a glare and cover little Jeremiah's ears. "I'd rather not send him back to Danielle swearing like a trucker."

"Don't worry about that," Danielle interjects, approaching the table, a coffee cup in hand. "He's heard it all, thanks to his uncles."

"Hi, Mrs. Lawrence," Claire says, standing and giving her a hug.

"How are you doing, dear? I hear you're no longer working the front desk at Holley Ridge."

"You hear correctly. Parker put me in charge of

marketing now that the renovations are done. You should see the place. It's stunning, but still has the same charm it did before. This Christmas will definitely be one for the history books. Parker's already planning it."

"Of course she is," Danielle says with a slight laugh.

The Holley Ridge Christmas festival is well-known all over the state for its holiday market and extravagant light display. Last year, the entire town worried it might be the last, since the property was on the brink of foreclosure and was being eyed by a real estate development firm as a prime location to build timeshares for all the wealthy snow birds who come this way to ski.

Thankfully, that same real estate developer fell in love with the property, and the owner of the quaint inn. He saved the place from foreclosure and spent the past several months helping to renovate it into the vision Parker had years ago when she inherited it from her parents. Now, it's become a premier wedding destination in the state, especially with the proximity to both Tahoe and Reno.

"Well, I promised this little guy a trip to the park before his morning nap." Danielle reaches for Jeremiah.

I stand, allowing her to take him. The ease with which she manages to carry him and balance her coffee is remarkable. After raising five kids, it's probably second nature.

"It was good seeing you, Danielle," I tell her.

"You, too, dear. I'm sure we'll be at the library next week for story time."

"Looking forward to it."

I give Jeremiah's hand a squeeze goodbye, then return to my chair, watching them leave.

"So what's going on?" Claire asks once we're alone. "Your text this morning sounded pretty urgent. Did you make a decision about…you know?" She gives me a knowing look.

"More like a decision was made for me."

She tilts her head, confusion knitting her brow. "I'm not sure I follow."

I take a long sip of coffee, then draw in a deep breath. "Finn saw my list."

"You mean *the* list?" She asks in a low voice.

I nod.

"What did you tell him?"

"The truth. I wasn't going to hide this from him. I *do* plan on hopefully getting pregnant and having a baby. Pretty sure he'd figure it out when I started to show."

"What did he say?"

I chew on my lower lip. "He poked fun at some of the names. In the end, he told me if this is what I want, he'll support me every step of the way. But then…" I trail off.

"Yes?" Claire perks up.

"He stopped by last night."

"And?"

"He told me I forgot a name." I pause, then add, "His."

Her eyes widen as my words ring out around us, seeming to drown out the whirring of the espresso machine and the clanging of forks against plates.

"What are you going to do?"

"I don't know," I sigh, shaking my head. "Over the past few days, I've been second guessing myself. Not the part about having a baby, but the part about *how* I go about getting pregnant. While it's expensive, it's probably less stressful to use an anonymous donor instead. But then Finn showed up offering to father my child, and now it's all I can think about."

"You could save tens of thousands of dollars this way," Claire reminds me.

"I know," I exhale. "It's not like I'm raking it in as the head librarian in a small town. I'm comfortable, but I don't have a pile of money stashed away. It's possible I could spend my entire savings and still have no baby to show for it."

"So you're going to tell him yes?" she prods, her eyes gleaming with enthusiasm.

"I don't know," I say again. "If I want to go about this naturally, I need to choose someone I trust completely. And Finn's the only man I *do* trust."

Hell, he's probably the only man I've *ever* trusted.

A sad thought, considering I was married for six years. But I never felt the level of comfort with Ethan I always have with Finn.

"Then what's the problem?" Claire presses.

"What if it ruins everything?"

"Set some ground rules. Keep things clear and simple. No lines crossed."

I let out a humorless laugh. "Lines tend to blur pretty quickly when sex is involved."

"Then make them un-blurrable," Claire replies. "Tell him your expectations so there's no confusion."

In theory, it sounds good. I'm just not sure if I have the ability to flip the switch like that. To separate things.

With anyone else, it probably wouldn't be a problem. But Finn's…different. He's *always* been different, even if I've never admitted it to anyone. It's probably one of the reasons my marriage failed. That and the fact my husband fell in love with someone else. But there was never that spark between us. Sex with Ethan was like vanilla ice cream. Reliable, familiar, but never surprising.

I have a feeling it would be completely different with Finn. He'd be more like chocolate molten lava cake. Decadent and indulgent, with a fiery center that promises something unexpected and thrilling. Something you grow to crave long after that last bite.

"Earth to Gen," Claire sings, pulling me out of my thoughts. Or, more appropriately, my fantasies.

"Sorry. I... It's a lot to think about." I take another sip of coffee.

"I bet it *is* a lot." She gives me a conniving smile as she waggles her brows.

"I'm being serious here," I whine. "There's a lot more at stake with Finn than any of the other names on my list."

"True, but I think this is the right move. You're not interested in the hassle of dating or marriage, right?"

"After Ethan, that ship has most definitely sailed."

"Then why not have a baby with your best friend?"

"I won't be having a baby *with* him," I correct quickly. "He'll just be getting me pregnant. There's a big difference."

"All the more reason for you to set up some ground rules. That way, you both know your expectations, as well as any…limitations."

I bring my cup to my lips and take another long sip, my mind spinning as I peer into the distance.

"Do you think I should tell him yes?" I ask, desperate for advice.

"I can't make that decision for you, Gen. But I know how much you've always dreamed of having kids. Finn's offering you a chance to have that without all the unnecessary complications that go along with marriage. If I were in your shoes, I'd take some time and really think about what your hard limits are, so to speak. If he's in agreement, I don't see any reason why you shouldn't accept his offer. You have everything to gain and nothing to lose."

Except my best friend if this blows up in our faces, I think to myself.

SEVEN

Finn

With two cups of coffee in hand, I make my way up the steps of the library, much like I've done countless times before. But today, it feels different.

For almost two weeks, I've been bracing for some sort of fallout from my proposition. I worried I'd completely destroyed our friendship by suggesting I be the one to get Genevieve pregnant.

But the very next day, she showed up at the fire station like nothing had changed, armed with a basket of freshly baked muffins that disappeared in minutes.

Since then, she hasn't mentioned a single word about it… In nearly two weeks.

I started to think maybe I'd imagined the whole thing.

But when I got a text from her this morning, asking if I could stop by to discuss a few things, I knew I didn't.

The library is quiet when I step inside, the scent of books and old wood filling the air. Mrs. Hudson, one of Genevieve's volunteers, waves at me from the historical fiction section, but she's too busy helping someone to stop and talk.

I give her a polite nod and continue down a long hallway, not stopping until I reach the office at the end. The door is open, and Genevieve's seated behind her desk, focused on her computer screen.

As if able to sense my presence, she glances up, her eyes locking on mine as a nervous smile tugs on her mouth.

"Finn. Hey." She stands, her chair scraping against the floor as she skirts around the desk to greet me.

"Hey." I lean down and brush a soft kiss to her cheek. As I do, I inhale the familiar scent of her — vanilla and something floral I can't name but always associate with her.

Pulling back, my gaze sweeps over her, taking in the way her jeans hug her curves, her black top dipping just low enough to have my imagination working on overtime.

Soon, she'll have even more curves. Her chest will be even fuller. Her hips softer. The thought hits me hard, and I fight to shake it off.

Because if that happens, I hope to God it's my baby she's carrying.

Which is insane.

A few weeks ago, the idea of being a father was the furthest thing from my mind.

Then again, Genevieve doesn't want me to be a father. She's only interested in my DNA.

At least, I *hope* she wants my DNA.

"Is one of those mine?" She gestures to the coffee cups in my hand.

I blink away my drifting thoughts and hand her one. "Americano with steamed two percent and one sweetener."

"You know me so well."

"I'd hope so by now." I smirk.

She takes a sip, then quietly closes the office door before returning to her seat. I settle into the chair across from her, the desk a sturdy barrier between us.

Her office is welcoming and organized, an outward expression of what's most important to her. Framed photos are scattered across the desk and shelves, mostly of her with her mom and sister, though there's one of the two of us from the Founder's Day Festival a few years ago. I smile at the memory of her nailing the dunk tank target, plunging me into a pool of cold water. A stack of books sits on the corner of her desk, the titles ranging from classic literature to steamy romance. One in particular catches my attention.

"*My Alien Bosses*?" I ask.

"It was Grandma Estelle's turn to pick this month's book club selection."

"Say no more." I chuckle under my breath, all too familiar with Grandma Estelle's affinity for some of the more risqué romance books.

She's a well-loved fixture here in Sycamore Falls. It's why all the locals refer to her as Grandma Estelle, even though she's never had children of her own. Considering she taught in the public school here for over forty years before she retired, she's more than made up for it.

But I'll never get over the fact that the woman who once taught me the difference between plural and possessive nouns likes to read books about aliens getting it on.

"What's on your mind?" I ask as I take a sip of my coffee.

"That's a loaded question," she mutters underneath her breath.

"As your friend, I get to ask the loaded questions."

"True." She lifts her eyes to mine for a lingering moment. Then she opens a desk drawer and pulls out a folder, sliding it across to me. "Here."

I raise an eyebrow, setting my coffee down and reaching for it. "What's this?"

"A pre-natal agreement," she responds, her voice calm but tight. "It's not legally binding, but it can be used as evidence if there are any future disputes. You can have your lawyer review it if you want."

I glance over the papers before returning my eyes to hers. "Does this mean you're accepting my offer?"

"As long as you agree to the terms." She straightens her posture. "I don't want the fact that we're friends to…muddy the waters. I want to be a mother without the complications of there being a father, so if you have any grand notions of undertaking a fatherly role because of our existing friendship, I'm sorry to disappoint you. You can still be in the child's life. I'd *expect* you to be since you're an important person in *my* life. But you won't be his or her father. I'd prefer no one know who the father is. My child included."

I swallow hard, feeling the weight of her words on my chest. I knew before offering to help I'd have no role in her child's life, apart from being his or her mother's best friend. But it still stings more than I expected.

"You want my DNA. Nothing more."

"Nothing more," she confirms, though there's a flicker of something in her expression. Something I can't quite explain.

Or maybe I'm just seeing things I *want* to see.

Without looking through the agreement, I grab a pen from her desk and sign the last page.

"Finn!" she exclaims. "What are you doing?"

"Signing this."

"You didn't even read it."

"I trust you," I tell her simply. "If this is what you want, I'll do whatever I need to help you."

She stares at me, stunned, before shaking her head with a small laugh. "You're impossible."

"Maybe." I flash her a sly grin before my expression turns sincere. "But I'm also all in."

"Thank you." She sighs, as if a giant weight has been lifted off her shoulders. Then she clears her throat and pulls out another piece of paper from her desk drawer, pushing it toward me.

"What's this?" I ask, picking it up.

"I thought it best to come up with some ground rules for…everything else."

"Everything else?" I arch a brow.

"The agreement you signed covers my expectations during pregnancy and after the baby's born. I thought it would be in our best interests to have guidelines in place to cover my expectations *before* I get pregnant.

"So… Regarding sex."

She blanches slightly, but quickly shakes it off, holding her head high. It's typical Genevieve. As long as I've known her, she's been confident and tenacious, even in situations that scare the shit out of her.

"Yes."

"Okay." I lean back in my chair and sip on my coffee as I read the first rule. "No outside partners."

"Since we'll be having unprotected sex, it goes

without saying that, for the duration of this, we only have sex with each other." She looks my way but doesn't meet my eyes. "Will that be a problem?"

"Nope," I declare firmly.

She arches a brow, parting her lips, and I can sense her wanting to push the issue.

But it's not an issue.

I don't tell her that the idea of being with any other women has lost its appeal since I discovered her list. She doesn't need to know that.

"Next rule," I declare, scanning her neat hand-writing. "Sex will occur once a day limited to the window of ovulation with a one-day buffer on either side."

"I know it may not be possible with your work schedule but—"

"I have plenty of PTO. If you give me the dates, I'll request off."

"You'd take time off from work for this?"

"This is important to you. So… Yes."

"Thanks."

I give her a slight smile, then return my attention to her list. "No physical intimacy outside of what's necessary."

"That way we don't complicate our friendship. If I'm not ovulating, there's no sex."

"That seems reasonable," I assure her as I continue reading, "Honesty at all times." I meet her eyes. "That won't be a problem. I'm always honest with you anyway."

"Me, too."

"Either party can back out for any reason, no questions asked," I say, reading the final rule on her list.

"If either of us wants to pull the plug, it ends and we forget it ever happened."

For some reason, hearing those words come out of Genevieve's mouth hits me harder than I expected. It's not like I've never had sex with a woman knowing it wouldn't go anywhere.

The same is true here.

It's just sex.

Nothing more.

Except Genevieve's a friend. My best friend.

All the more reason this could be a disaster.

But it's not enough for me to back down. Not when the mere idea of her asking someone else causes a vice to squeeze my chest.

"Agreed." I set the list back on her desk. "When do we start?"

She blinks repeatedly, obviously surprised by my agreement to all her conditions. I meant what I told her. This is important to her. I'll agree to anything she wants to be the one to give it to her.

"Based on my last cycle, I should start ovulating around the twentieth. So with the one-day buffer, we should start on the nineteenth."

"So…in 6 days.

She runs her hands down her jeans. "Yes."

"Is there a specific time of day that's better or—"

"Sperm can survive inside a woman's body for up to five days. As long as those swimmers are healthy when an egg is released, we're good to go."

"Good." I exhale a nervous breath, all of this starting to feel much more real than it did even seconds ago as we discussed her rules.

In six days, I'll be having sex with my best friend.

I can only hope she's still my best friend when this is all over.

EIGHT

Genevieve

I swipe a mascara wand over my lashes, capping the tube with a click before leaning in closer to the mirror. My reflection stares back at me, a little too wide-eyed and anxious for my liking.

"It's just Finn," I whisper under my breath.

But tonight, it isn't just Finn, my best friend.

It's Finn, the man who I'm about to have sex with so I can get pregnant.

"Nervous?" Claire asks as she lounges on my bed, her analytical gaze studying me from over her phone.

"I'm fine," I lie, forcing a smile.

"You don't seem fine."

"It's not a big deal," I reply, unsure if it's more for me or her.

Exhaling a long breath, she stands and walks

toward me, leaning against my vanity and crossing her arms in front of her chest.

"You don't have to pretend with me. You're about to sleep with Finn. *Your best friend.* I'd say that qualifies as a pretty big deal. It's okay to feel a little conflicted about it."

"I just… I don't want to turn it into something it's not. This is just a necessary prerequisite so I can have a baby. No feelings. No drama. Just sex."

"And you're ready for this? Crossing this line with him?"

I bite my bottom lip, my gaze dropping to the floor.

Am I ready?

That question has been echoing in my mind all day, no matter how hard I've tried to push it aside.

When I accepted Finn's offer and we set our plan in motion, six days seemed like a sufficient amount of time to mentally prepare myself for this.

But those six days went by much faster than I thought they would.

I keep reminding myself *why* I'm doing this. As long as I keep that goal in mind, maybe I won't be so nervous.

"I want a baby, Claire. I've waited long enough now, and I'm not getting any younger. Finn's agreed to everything I need. Every rule, every condition. It's just sex. Easy, meaningless sex."

She gives me a skeptical look. She doesn't need to

say the words for me to know what she's thinking. That with Finn, it would never be meaningless. Not when he's one of the most important people in my life.

Thankfully, she doesn't voice her concerns. Instead, she wraps me in a tight hug.

"You're going to be an amazing mom." She pulls back, her eyes locking with mine. "And you're doing this for the right reasons. Don't forget that. Okay?"

Her words ease some of the tension coiled in my chest, and I let out a shaky exhale. "Thanks, Claire."

"Anytime." She gives me a sincere smile before her expression turns conniving. "For the record, I still think you're going to enjoy tonight way more than you're willing to admit."

I groan, swatting her arm. "Claire."

"What?" She laughs, grabbing her bag from my bed. "Finn's hot, and you've been friends for years. You two already have the kind of trust most couples dream of. If you ask me, having that level of comfort with someone makes things much more enjoyable in the bedroom."

"This isn't about enjoying myself in the bedroom," I remind her, pushing down the mental image of Finn and me together. Of him hovering over me. Of his muscles rippling as he's overcome with ecstasy. I have to suppress the whimper that wants to be set free.

"There's no shame in enjoying yourself. Your goal

may be to get pregnant, but you should also enjoy the journey, if you know what I mean." She waggles her brows, then turns from me, heading out of my bedroom.

"Call me tomorrow," she instructs as I follow her into the living room. "I want to hear how it went. Well, not *all* the details, but the general vibe."

"Okay," I agree as she gives me one last hug.

I watch the door shut behind her, the click echoing in the now-quiet house. Closing my eyes, I draw in a deep breath to calm my nerves.

"It's just sex," I whisper to myself on the exhale. "Nothing more."

I have a feeling I'll be reminding myself of this quite often over the coming days.

Suddenly, the doorbell rips through the space, causing my heart to skyrocket into my throat.

It's another reminder that tonight isn't a typical night. Finn never uses the doorbell. He usually just lets himself in.

Not tonight.

I take a slow breath, willing my pulse to settle as I step toward the door. My palms feel clammy, so I wipe them against my jeans before wrapping my fingers around the knob. Then I open the door and meet Finn's gaze, his signature crooked smile firmly in place.

Instead of the t-shirt and shorts he typically wears, he's in jeans and a button-down, the sleeves rolled up to reveal his forearms, his dark hair damp from a recent shower. I have no business noticing the way the fabric clings to his shoulders or how the open collar reveals a hint of tanned skin.

But I do.

And that realization sends a fresh wave of unease coursing through me.

"Hey," he says, his voice warm and familiar, though there's an edge to it.

"Hey." My response comes out slightly breathless, and I clear my throat as I step aside to let him in.

As he moves past me, the scent of his body wash wraps around me. The space between us suddenly feels smaller, the walls of my quaint cottage closing in.

I planned this whole thing meticulously. Took nearly two weeks to accept his offer because I wanted to explore every possible angle.

But now, standing here in the same space we've shared countless times, I realize I didn't plan for *this*. For the moment before we cross the point of no return.

"How are you?" Finn asks, breaking through the tense silence.

"Good," I reply, my voice not sounding like my own. "You?"

"Good." He rubs the back of his neck, the tension between us growing by the second. His gaze flickers toward mine, then away, then back again. I don't think I've ever seen him this unsure of himself.

Instead of making this even more awkward, I decide the best way is to just rip off the proverbial bandage.

"We should probably get to business then."

He pushes out a nervous laugh. "Wow. Okay. Direct."

"What else are we supposed to do?" I spin and head down the hallway, each step making my heart pound harder. "You're here to get me pregnant. May as well get on with it."

As I cross the threshold of my bedroom, I start to unbutton my jeans. But before I can lower the zipper, Finn wraps his hand around my forearm.

"Hold on a second, Genevieve."

I dart my eyes up to meet his, a look on his face I can't quite read.

"What's wrong? Are you changing your mind?" I ask, half joking, half serious. "It's okay if you are. It's in the ground rules."

"I'm not changing my mind. I just…" He drops his hold on me and scrubs a hand through his hair. "This feels…*weird*. Not because it's you," he adds quickly, his brows pulling together, "but because of how we're going about it. Like some clinical transaction. I don't know…" He sighs. "It just feels a little too *Handmaid's Tale* for me."

"Well, what do you suggest?" I plant my hands on my hips.

He steps closer, his expression softening. "Let's go

do something first. That way this will feel more…natural."

"The whole point of tonight is to try to get me pregnant. Not hang out."

"And we'll get to that," he says, his mouth twitching like he's trying not to smile. "This just… It doesn't feel like us."

He's not wrong. Going somewhere first, though? That feels dangerously close to a date.

But if it makes Finn feel more comfortable, it's the least I can do, considering what he's agreed to give me.

"What do you have in mind?"

"You'll see." He winks, and grabs my hand, his touch warm and steady as he tugs me out of my house.

NINE

Finn

"Mini golf?" Genevieve gives me a skeptical look as I pull into the parking lot of King Putt, a relic of our teen years with its mismatched concrete dinosaurs and tiki torches that flicker against the twilight.

"What did you think we'd do?" I jump out of my truck and meet her as she climbs down.

"I don't know." She shrugs. "Maybe go to Jude's brewery and have a few beers."

"I'd rather be sober for tonight," I tell her in a low voice, leaning in close.

A subtle breeze wraps around us, kicking up her familiar scent. A shiver rolls through her, but I get the feeling it has nothing to do with the temperature, considering it's a comfortable seventy degrees.

"This place has always been good for thinking about something else for a little while. Just don't be upset when I kick your ass." I throw her a playful smirk as we make our way toward the entrance.

"You think so, Lawrence?"

"Most definitely, Thomas."

"Big talk for someone who cheats."

"I don't cheat. I strategize."

Genevieve rolls her eyes, and I steer her toward the counter. There's a short line, so I grab a couple of golf balls from the bins filled with balls of nearly every shade of the rainbow.

"Teal for you."

She arches a brow as she takes the ball from me. "Did you just assume my color preference?"

"Teal's been your favorite color since you were fourteen and declared pink was dead to you," I remind her. "Don't start pretending to like something else now."

She shakes her head but smiles anyway, tossing the ball into the air and catching it. "It's always been my lucky color."

"You'll need quite a bit of luck if you hope to stand a chance against me."

"We'll see about that."

I pay for both of us, despite Genevieve's protest, then grab our clubs.

The mini golf course is buzzing tonight — parents wrangling kids, teenagers in awkward date territory, and a group of moms chatting near the third hole while their kids run wild. The faint scent of fresh grass mixes with chlorine from the decorative waterfall, and the tiki torches crackle faintly in the breeze. Overhead, the last streaks of pink fade into a deep indigo sky.

A wave of memories washes over me as I take it all in, this night reminding me of another from years ago.

After my dad finally succumbed to the ALS that plagued him for years, Genevieve dragged me here, even though it was the last thing I wanted to do. At least that's what I thought at the time.

We played the whole course without saying a word. She didn't ask me how I was doing after losing the most important person in my life, unlike everyone else. But Genevieve's never been like everyone else. She always knew when I didn't want to talk. When I needed to think about something other than hospitals and empty chairs at dinner tables. When I just needed to breathe.

Over the years, that's exactly what mini golf has become for us. A place to breathe.

It's where I took her when she moved back after her divorce. It's where she takes me after I've had a difficult call at work. I figure it's what we both need tonight, too.

"You've got an audience." Genevieve's voice pulls me out of my memories.

"What are you talking about?"

She nods toward the group of moms ignoring their kids on hole three.

I glance over and, sure enough, the group of married women are definitely checking me out. One even waves when she catches my eye.

"Great."

"Didn't she make the winning bid on you during the Founders Day auction last year?" Genevieve taunts with a smirk, referring to the platinum blonde at the center of the group.

"She didn't bid on *me*. She bid on the *experience* I offered," I correct.

The Founders Day Festival is an annual tradition in Sycamore Falls, celebrating the founding of our small town nearly a hundred and fifty years ago during the gold rush days. As a way to raise money for the local community center that provides assistance to those in need, there's an auction where locals can bid on experiences to do with people in town. Breakfast with the mayor. A day of home improvement with a local handyman. My brother, Jude, even offers a beer-making class.

While most people bid on the experience they're interested in without a single thought about *who's* offering it, some bid because of that precise reason. Like Chassidy Monroe last year.

Even though she's married.

That didn't stop her from wearing a skin tight

dress as I inspected her house for potential fire hazards.

"I bet you gave her quite the experience. She was talking about the *experience* for weeks after. Every time she came in the library, she'd tell everyone who listened how *transcendental* it was."

"I did a fire inspection of her house and made recommendations to reduce her risk of fire."

"Maybe fire safety is her kink."

I shake my head, trying to ignore the way my body responds to hearing Genevieve talk about kinks. It makes me wonder if she has any kinks.

Would she be timid and shy? Would she be determined to remain in control? Or would she be adventurous?

"The only reason she won is because you refused to bid on me," I tell her, not wanting to dwell too long on what Genevieve's kinks may be. "I mean, my services."

Her grin widens. "Hey, I'm not made of money. Plus, I didn't want to bruise your ego by bidding five bucks."

"Real supportive, Gen." I playfully nudge her, thankful to have this version of her back. Not the woman overrun with nerves over the prospect of sleeping with her best friend.

"Someone's got to keep you humble."

"I'm glad it's you."

She holds my gaze for a beat, something shifting

between us. Then she quickly spins around before it can build into something more, dropping her ball onto the green.

As she lines up her shot, she bends slightly, and my focus snags on the curve of her hips. I swallow hard, dragging my gaze upward, but it's too late. I've already noticed the way her jeans cling to her in all the right places, including the sliver of skin where her shirt rides up as she shifts.

Finally, she takes her shot, and I exhale, thankful for the distraction. The ball rolls down the green, stopping just shy of the hole.

"Dammit," she curses under her breath.

"Better luck next time. Now let a real pro show you how it's done."

She crosses her arms over her chest, pushing her breasts up in a way that's downright distracting. "Oh, really?"

"Really."

I purposefully avoid looking at her as I line up my shot, praying I don't fuck it up. But instead of the smooth, controlled stroke I intend, the ball ricochets off a plastic dinosaur and lands in the rough.

Genevieve throws her head back and laughs, the sound sinking straight into my chest.

"Is that how it's done?" she teases. "I thought the point of mini golf was to avoid the obstacles."

"It was a warm-up shot."

"Sure. Take as many warm-up shots you need."

After four painful attempts, I finally sink the ball, and we move through the course, our banter easy, the tension between us settling into something familiar. When she misses an easy shot, I poke fun at her. When she sinks a hole-in-one, she throws her arms around me in celebration. It's just like every other time we've been here.

Except it's not.

"Who won?" Genevieve asks after she sinks her ball into the last hole and it disappears down the chute.

I tally up the scorecard, then wrinkle my brow.

"It's me, isn't it?" she presses, a triumphant lilt in her voice.

I blink repeatedly, certain I must have added wrong. I never lose to Genevieve.

Then again, I've been pretty distracted all night. I thought mini golf would be a safe bet, something to relax her.

But every time she lined up her shot, giving me a perfect view of her ass, I couldn't stop thinking about what we'd be doing *after* we left here.

"Maybe," I answer nonchalantly.

"Are you serious?" She snatches the scorecard out of my hand.

"Don't let it go to your head. You got lucky. It won't happen again."

"We'll see about that." She laughs.

I love seeing her like this — flushed from victory,

eyes bright, confidence radiating from her. It's exactly what I wanted when I insisted we get out of her house. But what happens when we *do* go back to her house? Will the tension be back?

I know it will. Unless I do something to break it down first. To burst through the wall that's always existed between us.

Before I can talk myself out of it, I grab her hand and tug her behind the large windmill.

"Finn, what are you—"

I don't give her time to finish. To overthink. To put space between us.

Instead, I press my lips to hers.

She stiffens immediately, her hands pushing against my chest. It's not a shove. More of a warning. A hesitation.

I feel it in the way she presses against me. In the way her lips remain still. In the way her muscles tighten.

She's resisting.

But it's not just me she's fighting. It's herself. Her damn rules. The ones I have no business breaking, but I can't stop myself.

Cupping her jaw, I angle her head and deepen the kiss, my tongue sweeping over the seam of her lips, coaxing them to part.

She inhales sharply.

A breath.

A shutter.

And then, finally, she surrenders to me.

Her fingers twist in my shirt, clutching me like she's afraid I'll pull away now that she's opened to me.

She's wrong.

I want more. So much more.

Digging my fingers into her hair, I take control of the kiss. Of *her*.

Her lips part for me, and the second our tongues meet, a quiet, breathy whimper spills from her throat. The sound punches through me, slamming straight to my gut.

Fuck.

That sound shouldn't undo me like this.

I shouldn't react this way. It's just a whimper. Just a kiss.

I've kissed plenty of women. Heard countless whimpers just like that.

But this… This is different.

This is *Genevieve*.

And somehow, my body knows it.

I slide my free hand down the curve of her frame, my fingers flexing at her waist. It takes everything in me to resist the urge to pin her against the windmill. To press into her. Let her feel exactly what that innocent sound does to me.

I force myself to slow down. To ease back before I lose control.

But when I pull away, I don't let go. My hands

remain on her, my thumbs grazing the rapid pulse at the base of her throat. Her chest rises and falls in time with mine, our breathing uneven, unsteady.

Her lips are swollen. From me. The sight triggers something dark and possessive inside me. Something I shouldn't like as much as I do.

"Ready to go home now?" I manage to ask, my voice rough and thick with restraint.

I half expect her to berate me for breaking the rules, to remind me this wasn't part of our arrangement.

Instead, she swallows hard and gives a quick nod. "Yes."

I don't hesitate. I grasp her hand and all but drag her out of here before she can change her mind.

TEN

Genevieve

My body tingles as I sit in the front seat of Finn's truck, still breathless, my mind reeling from his kiss. Every inch of me is on high alert, desperate to feel his lips on mine again.

And maybe other places, too.

I knew things with Finn would be intense. There's always been an attraction simmering between us, no matter how hard I tried to ignore it. And I did try. Because deep down, I knew once I had a taste, I'd never be satisfied with anyone else.

That kiss just proved it.

And it was only a kiss. A sensual tease.

A silent promise of what's to come.

The ten-minute drive stretches into eternity, the air between us thick with unspoken words and unfulfilled need. My fingers curl against my thighs, desperate for something, *anything*, to ground me. But nothing does.

Not when Finn is sitting mere inches away, gripping the wheel with white-knuckled tension, his jaw tight, chest rising and falling a little too fast.

He feels it, too.

When he pulls into my driveway and cuts the engine, silence settles between us. Not awkward. Not uncertain. Just charged.

Neither of us speaks as we step out of the truck. I move toward the front door, entering the code with shaky fingers. Finn follows me inside, shutting the door behind him with a click. The sound echoes in the quiet house, and when I face him, something in his expression shifts.

I step closer, drawn to him by some unseen force, the atmosphere heavy with anticipation. My heart pounds, my breathing growing shallow as I tilt my head back.

He doesn't move. Doesn't close the distance. He lets me be the one to cross the line.

I wet my lips, my voice barely above a whisper as I beg, "Kiss me, Finn."

He swipes his tongue along his bottom lip, his blue eyes flaming with lust. Then he cups my cheeks, his thumbs brushing against my skin.

His palms are warm, rough, and slightly unsteady, like he's barely holding himself together. With a deep, ragged groan, his mouth crashes against mine, and heat surges through my veins, pooling low in my stomach.

He takes his time at first. Teasing. Testing. Tempting.

But when our tongues collide, a moan slips from my throat, and Finn loses control.

His grip tightens, his body pressing my back against the wall, one hand sliding down my waist to anchor me in place. Every inch of him — his heat, his strength, the raw hunger in the way he kisses me — ignites something deep inside me.

I want more.

I *need* more.

I curl my fingers into his shirt, pulling him closer, but it's not enough. Nothing ever will be again.

Finn rips his mouth from mine, breathing hard, chest heaving. His eyes are wild, dark with something I've never seen before. Something dangerously close to possession.

"Am I that bad of a kisser?" I tease, trying to break the tension, but my voice is breathless, unsteady.

"Just the opposite." He shakes his head as if trying to clear it. "I had a feeling it would be good. But I didn't expect it to be like this."

"Like what?" I rise onto my toes, my lips hovering over his.

He digs his fingers into my hair. "Like I'm ready

to lose my damn mind if I'm not inside you in the next few minutes."

I shiver, my entire body humming with anticipation. "Then what are you waiting for?"

Another groan rumbles from his chest. Then his mouth is back on mine, his kiss deeper, hungrier, like he's starved for this.

For me.

With a firm grip on my hips, he guides me backward down the hall, his lips never leaving mine, maneuvering the path as if he's walked it dozens of times.

He has, but never with the intention of having sex with me.

That all changes tonight.

When my legs hit the bed, Finn slowly pulls back to meet my gaze. Now that we're in my softly lit bedroom and mere seconds away from actually doing this, a fresh surge of nerves floods over me.

I'm not sure what I'm more nervous about… Ruining our friendship or Finn seeing too much of me. More than just physically.

"Genevieve."

His husky voice tugs me back from my thoughts, grounding me in the present.

"Get out of your head."

I huff a soft laugh. Of course, he knows exactly where my mind has gone. He always does. That should be comforting, but it makes me feel even more vulnerable.

"Sorry." I give him a sheepish smile. "It's been a while since I've done this."

His expression softens, a flicker of something unreadable crossing his face. "Then let me remind you what it's like."

His lips find mine again, softer this time. More patient. He lowers me onto the mattress, and his warmth presses into me, surrounding me. Every touch, every brush of his fingers against my skin is deliberate. He's not rushing. He's savoring. And somehow, that makes this even more intense.

"Finn," I whisper, my breath catching as his hands skim over me, tracing familiar yet foreign paths over my body.

He plants soft, lingering kisses along my jawline as he works his way to the sensitive curve of my neck.

"You smell like vanilla." His voice is low, rough with restraint. "Always have."

His words send a rush of warmth through me, the kind that has nothing to do with desire and everything to do with the fact that he remembers. That he's noticed. That even when I thought he only saw me as his best friend, he was paying attention.

He slips a hand beneath my shirt, my pulse increasing as he nears my breast. When he cups it, I gasp, my core aching with need.

"I've imagined what these would feel like since the

summer I was fifteen and saw you in a bikini," he confesses with a playful lilt in his tone.

"Is that right?" I give him a coy smile.

"Most definitely." He meets my eyes. "I had to go jerk off so you wouldn't see the tent in my fucking swim trunks."

A renewed wave of excitement crashes over me, and I thread my fingers through his hair, arching toward him. "If you think they feel good, why don't you have a taste?"

He responds by slamming his lips to mine, tightening his grip around my breast, my nerve endings on fire. Without missing a beat, he briefly pulls away to remove my shirt. I help him, needing his mouth on me like I need my next breath.

I didn't foresee tonight going like this. I didn't anticipate there being much in the way of foreplay. That's not what this is supposed to be about. It was supposed to be just sex. But these next few days may be the only time I'll get to experience him like this. I may as well enjoy everything he's willing to give me.

Finn tosses my shirt onto the floor, then reaches behind me, unclasping my bra with the efficiency of someone who's done it quite a few times. Returning to me, he brushes his mouth against mine before trailing a path down my frame. The heat of his breath on my skin sets me on fire, every lingering kiss stoking the flames even more.

When he circles his tongue along my nipple, I

moan in surrender, my body a slave to this man's touch.

"Fucking perfect," Finn remarks in a husky, reverent tone as he continues worshiping me. "Your tits are fucking perfect, Genevieve." He takes my nipple back into his mouth, alternating between tender sucking and gentle nibbling.

I don't know how much more of this I can take. I'm wound tighter than I have been in years. Maybe ever. I don't remember it being like this with Ethan.

Then again, Ethan never brought any of these emotions out of me. There were no passionate declarations of love. No unrelenting need. Instead, the reason I chose Ethan is because he was reliable. Safe.

Finn is anything but safe, in more ways than one.

But that's not enough of a reason for me to put a stop to this. To tell him I'm only interested in getting pregnant. Not any of this extra stuff.

Because this extra stuff is fucking incredible.

He moves deliberately, showering my stomach with kisses while his tongue traces lazy circles around my belly button. The roughness of his unshaven jawline against my skin makes the ache between my legs grow even more prominent.

When he reaches the button on my jeans, I draw in a shaky breath, my muscles tightening.

"Relax, Gen," he soothes, leaving a trail of kisses along the waistband. "I want to make this good for you."

"You already have." My words leave me before I can stop them.

He lifts his gaze to mine, a cocky smirk tugging on his lips. "Then let me make it even better." He arches a brow, silently asking permission.

I quickly nod.

His focused gaze remains locked on mine as he unbuttons my jeans and lowers the zipper. I lift my hips, allowing him to drag my pants down my legs, along with my panties.

His pupils dilate as he rakes his gaze over my body for what feels like an excruciatingly long time. I can't help but feel somewhat self-conscious, especially since I know how in shape Finn is, all hard ridges and defined edges. I don't look like that.

But by the way he admires me, you'd think I was the most alluring woman he's ever seen.

"Fucking beautiful," he murmurs as he touches his lips against mine. "You are so damn beautiful, Genevieve."

I melt into his kiss, doing everything in my power to remind myself this isn't real. He's probably just saying these things to get me in the mood. Or maybe to get *himself* in the mood.

Although, if memory serves, he's been in the mood since that kiss at the mini golf course.

He snakes down my body again, his tongue leaving no inch of me unexplored.

As he moves lower and lower, my pulse increases,

my breathing growing even more ragged. Not out of nerves, but from anticipation.

When he finally settles between my legs, I'm on the brink of combusting.

One thing is certain. Finn is a master of foreplay. I've never been so damn turned on before in my life. So ready to fall over the edge. Instead of constantly thinking how weird it should feel to be doing this with Finn, the thought hasn't even entered my mind. All I can think about is how desperate I am for his touch. It's as if he knows exactly where to touch, kiss, and suck to push my body higher and higher.

"Is this for me?" he asks.

"What?" I pant, struggling to catch my breath.

Biting his lower lip, he drags a finger along my slick center, gently rubbing my clit.

I close my eyes and moan, the intensity of his touch sending ripples of pleasure through me. It's been over a year since anyone's touched me there. Maybe longer.

Ethan and I were never the type of couple who couldn't keep our hands off each other. In the beginning, especially after I finally gave my virginity to him, we had sex quite a bit. But over time, it sort of fizzled out to the point where we would go weeks, sometimes months, without having sex. It almost felt like more of a chore.

That's not the case with Finn. Nothing about this feels like a chore at all.

"This, Genevieve. How fucking soaked you are." He continues torturing me as he hovers over me, taking in my entire body. Then he lowers his mouth to within a breath of mine. "Tell me it's all for me."

I don't even hesitate. I can't. This man has turned me into a puppet, a willing marionette dancing for him. Only him.

"It's all for you," I whimper.

He presses his mouth more firmly against mine. "Good girl."

Holy shit.

I've read romance books where the hero calls the heroine a good girl. But nothing could have prepared me for how it would feel to have someone murmur those words to me in real life.

And not just anyone.

But Finn Lawrence.

He moves down my body again, his fingers still teasing my clit. The lower he gets, the more tightly wound I become, anticipation coiling inside me like a snake.

"Finn," I moan, desperate for something, *anything*, to dull this unbearable ache.

"Yes?"

"I need you inside me."

"And I'm desperate to be inside you. But first I need to taste you." He returns his stare to mine, something harsh and demanding within. "So spread your legs and let me taste your pussy."

ELEVEN

Genevieve

*F*uck. *Me.*

I had a feeling Finn would have a sexy bedroom voice, but I never thought I'd hear it directed at me. I thought he'd save it for someone he actually wants to sleep with. Not someone he's only doing this with because I want a baby.

It wasn't supposed to be like this. It was supposed to be easy. Transactional.

Which is probably why my body tenses as he pushes my thighs apart, his mouth inches from the spot I'm desperate to feel him, but scared at the same time.

"Relax, Gen," he soothes, his voice deep and patient, like he has all the time in the world. "Let me make you feel good." Pausing, he flicks his gaze to mine. "Are you okay with me doing this?"

A nervous laugh escapes my throat. "I think so."

"You *think* so?"

"It's just…" I bite my lower lip, feeling more vulnerable than I expected.

He pushes himself up until he's face-to-face with me again, cupping my cheek. His touch is steady, grounding.

"Remember the rules. Complete honesty. It's the only way this works." He pushes a tendril of hair away from my face. "You can tell me anything."

"I know." I briefly close my eyes, drawing in a shaky breath. When I return my gaze to his, I admit, "I've never done this."

He furrows his brow. "What? Sex?"

"No," I answer quickly. "I've had sex before. I *was* married for six years."

Something flickers in his expression. Something sharp and unreadable. His jaw tightens, as if the reminder of my marriage unsettles him.

"I've never done *this*." I give him a knowing look, hoping he'll pick up on what I'm trying to say.

His furrow deepens before realization washes over him and his eyes widen. "You're telling me you were married to that prick for six years and, in that entire time, he never went down on you?"

I shrug. "He said he didn't like the taste."

Finn stares at me for what feels like an eternity,

my admission hanging heavy in the air. Finally, he says, "He's a bigger idiot than I thought." He shakes his head, then refocuses his intense stare on me. "Tell me something, Genevieve. Did he ever make you come?"

I try to avert my gaze, but he won't let me, his hold firm, his eyes demanding nothing but the truth.

"Did he?"

My throat works around a swallow, and I give a small shake of my head.

Finn exhales through his nose, a slow, controlled breath, but the tension in his body tells me he's anything but calm. A slow, devilish smile tugs at the corners of his lips, half amused, half something else entirely.

"Then I guess I have some work to do," he murmurs, lowering his mouth to mine. "And since I only have a few days, I better get started."

Before I can respond, he presses one last kiss to my lips, then leisurely trails his mouth down my body, as if committing every inch to memory.

By the time he settles between my thighs again, I'm trembling. Not with nerves. But with need.

He drags a hand between my legs, spreading my slickness around, his gaze locked on mine. "Do you trust me?"

"Yes," I whisper, the words barely audible yet filled with unwavering certainty.

His smile softens, something warm and knowing

shining in his eyes. "Then let me show you how good it can be."

I hold my breath, each second stretching as I wait to feel his mouth on my most sensitive spot. Finally, I feel it — a slow, deliberate swipe of his tongue as it drags upward and lands on my clit. A rush of exhilaration overwhelms me, and a deep, uncontrollable moan escapes my throat.

I've never felt anything like this before. Ethan had touched me on occasion. Tried to get me off that way. But after enduring several minutes of him rubbing my clit like it was a stubborn stain he was trying to get rid of, I usually faked an orgasm so it would be over.

But this? I don't want this to be over anytime soon.

"So fucking delicious," Finn groans against me. "I can eat you for hours."

Each word is a sensual promise that sends sparks through me. I'm overwhelmed with sensation, chasing my release but also not wanting it to end.

It's a surprising thought, considering my original plan that we'd have sex for a few minutes, then go back to the way things typically were. Now, with each swirl of his tongue igniting something deep inside me, I don't want him to ever stop. I'm drowning in him, my sole focus on the delicious pleasure he's able to so easily coax from me.

I slowly pulse my hips against him, my body

moving of its own volition. I'm held captive by him, my mind focused on one thing only — feeling good.

"That's right, baby. Fuck my face."

"Oh, god," I exhale. Desperation courses through me, a wildfire ignited by his touch and fanned by his words.

I grip the sheets below me, needing something to keep me grounded when I feel like I'm soaring, flying, being catapulted into oblivion.

"Don't fight it, Gen," Finn grunts, increasing his motions. "Let yourself go. Let yourself feel." He inserts a finger inside me. "Let yourself feel *me*."

He returns his mouth to me at the same time as he adds another finger, and I'm lost. Utterly and completely lost.

"Finn!" His name is a cry, a benediction that echoes off the walls as the most intense orgasm I've ever experienced crashes over me. My body is a trembling, spasming mess, but he doesn't stop. He keeps going, wringing every last drop of pleasure from me.

When he finally straightens, his hair is mussed, lips quirked in a sexy, satisfied smile and glistening with my arousal.

"How was it?"

I tug him toward me, clutching his face in my hands. "Fucking incredible." I press my mouth against his and wrap my legs around his waist, the taste of me on him more of a turn on than I expected.

"There's plenty more where that came from."

"I hope so."

"Most definitely. If you think my mouth drives you wild, just wait until you feel my cock." His eyes darken, a wicked promise in their midnight depths.

"Then what are you waiting for?"

"You don't have to ask me twice." He touches another kiss to my mouth before crawling off the bed.

My eyes remain trained on his as he unbuttons his shirt and tosses it onto the floor, revealing broad shoulders, a sculpted chest, and a set of defined abs that ripple with every subtle movement. Don't even get me started on that enticing little V that disappears into his shorts. My mouth waters at the idea of dragging my tongue along each and every ridge.

This isn't the first time I've seen him without his shirt. But it's the first time I've allowed myself to truly drink in the sight of him. To savor the raw, undeniable magnetism he exudes.

He couldn't be any more different from Ethan if he tried.

Where Finn is fit and broad, Ethan was slender. He wasn't scrawny. More trim than anything.

But Finn… He's the embodiment of sex appeal. And the scattered tattoos decorating his chest and biceps only add to his rugged allure.

Time seems to stand still as he lowers the zipper on his jeans and pushes them down his legs along with his boxers, his eyes trained on me the entire time. His legs are just as muscular as the rest of his body. And his cock... It's the cherry on top of an already remarkable package.

"Like what you see?" Smirking, he wraps his hand around his impressive erection and gives it a few tugs.

"It's…adequate." Although my voice betrays the truth. This man is far more than merely adequate.

A low chuckle rumbles from his chest as he crawls onto the bed, settling between my legs. When he teases my center, a moan involuntarily slips from my throat again.

"That doesn't sound like adequate to me, Gen," he murmurs, his warm breath ghosting against my mouth. "If you ask me, that moan sounds like you need to be fucked."

My pulse kicks up, his words igniting a heat that surges through me.

"Tell me," he grinds out, the tightness in his jaw making it clear he's struggling to maintain control.

"Tell you what?" I pant breathlessly, every fiber of my being trembling, making me think I might shatter the moment he slides into me.

"Tell me you need to be fucked." He teases me with his erection once more, then curves toward me, taking my bottom lip between his teeth. "Tell me you need me to fuck this cunt."

His words steal my breath, each syllable charged with a hunger I've never experienced. Sure, I've read quite a few romance novels where the hero has said something like this to the heroine and found myself turned on.

I never thought I'd experience it in real life.

"That's the reason you're here," I remind him, trying to break through the sexual tension.

But I doubt anything can.

And when Finn gives me a stern look, I know he has no intention of backing down from his request.

"Tell me, Genevieve." He slides his erection up and down my slickness, torturing me. "Tell me you need me to fuck you."

His gaze locks on me. I know he's not asking me to say this because he needs to hear the words. He's doing this because he senses I need this. Need to let loose for once in my life. Need to release my inhibitions.

"Finn…" I pant, gripping his face tightly. "I need you to fuck me."

"Thank god." He slams his mouth to mine in a heated kiss. But he doesn't thrust inside. Instead, he tears away and stands, continuing to stroke his erection.

"What are—" I begin to protest, but his commanding tone cuts me off.

"Hands and knees."

"Hands and knees?" I repeat.

"I read this position helps to increase chances of conception."

"You did?" I'm unable to hide my surprise over his admission.

"Yes. So hands and knees."

On a hard swallow, I obey his command, rolling over and propping myself up. When I feel the bed dip behind me, another bout of nervous butterflies flit low in my stomach.

"Relax," Finn soothes, bringing his arousal up to me.

I hitch a breath as he teases my opening.

"This is new to you, too, isn't it?"

I glance over my shoulder. "How did you know?"

"If Ethan wasn't willing to eat you out, I'd guess he wasn't too adventurous. Although I don't exactly consider this all that adventurous."

A part of me wants to ask what he *does* consider adventurous, but that's not the point of this arrangement.

Either was him going down on me, yet here we are.

"He liked what he liked," I attempt to argue on Ethan's behalf.

"Selfish bastard," Finn mutters under his breath. "What about what *you* like?"

"I don't really know what I like," I reply.

"Then let me help you figure it out."

He positions his erection at my opening again, and I immediately tense.

"Breathe, baby."

I do as he asks, drawing in a deep breath.

Then on my exhale, he thrusts into me.

TWELVE

Finn

Genevieve's screams reverberate through the room as I bury myself deep inside of her, clutching her hips as if my life depends on it. In a way, it feels like it does. I've never experienced anything as incredible as being inside of Genevieve. I knew she'd feel amazing. But I never expected it to be this damn explosive.

And knowing I'm the first person to give her an orgasm, the first person to taste her delicious pussy, the first person to fuck her like this fills me with a strange feeling. Not ownership. But a connection I wasn't anticipating.

Or maybe a connection I hoped I *wouldn't* feel.

Because at the end of the day, this won't change who we are to each other.

"You okay?" I murmur, scattering gentle kisses along the soft expanse of her shoulder blades.

"Y-yes. Just…overwhelmed."

"Good overwhelmed?" My voice is low as I brush my lips along her neck.

"A fucking incredible overwhelmed."

"Good to know." I chuckle, playfully nipping at her skin. "I'll take it easy on you and go slow. I'm guessing it's been a while."

"It has." She glances back at me, her eyes filled with hunger. "But I don't want you to go slow. That's all I've had. I don't want what I've always had. I want something new."

Her words send a rush of excitement through me.

Genevieve's always been direct, but I wasn't sure if it would transfer to the bedroom, especially with how nervous she's been.

"I can give you something new." I slowly retreat, the clenching of her walls around me making me teeter on the edge of losing control.

But I want this to last. Don't want this to end before it has to, especially when there's a possibility I'll only be able to do this for a few more days.

When I slam back into her, we both groan at the same time.

"You feel so damn good." I smooth my hands over her delicious curves and down her arms, linking my fingers with hers. When I nibble on the part of her neck where it meets her shoulder, she yelps, but it turns into a moan. "So damn warm." I slowly circle my hips. "So damn tight."

"More," she pleads as she wiggles against me. "Let me feel more of you."

"I'll always give you what you want." I dig my teeth harder into her flesh, sucking on it. Then I straighten, grabbing onto her hips again.

This time when I drive into her, there's no pause. No hesitation. I'm a man on a mission, propelled forward by the way being with this woman who knows me better than anyone else makes me feel.

I've had some pretty good sex, but it's never been like this.

All the more reason this is a horrible idea.

But it's too late to stop now.

I couldn't, even if I wanted to.

And I don't want to.

"Finn," Genevieve moans, her voice strained with anticipation and need.

"You're getting close, aren't you? I can feel your pussy getting tighter around me."

She doesn't say anything. Just grips the sheets even harder, her chest heaving through her uneven breaths.

"Touch yourself. Get yourself off all over my cock."

When she snaps her gaze to mine over her shoulder, I expect for her to tell me she doesn't feel comfortable doing that in front of me. I can read between the lines. She may not be a virgin, but she's pretty inexperienced when it comes to sex, especially if tonight was her first time having a guy go down on her and getting fucked doggie-style.

Then she curves her lips into a smile, resting her weight on one arm as she snakes her other hand down her torso, finding that little bundle of nerves and rubbing.

"Fuck," I hiss, relishing in the sensation.

She attempts to close her eyes, but before she can, I wrap my hand around her hair, forcing her gaze to meet mine through the mirror hanging over her bed.

"Keep your eyes on me. I want to look into them as you come. Want you to watch me fuck you."

I'm not sure what's come over me. I'm normally not this vocal in the bedroom. Sure, I do whatever necessary to make it good for both me and whoever I'm with, but this is at a completely different level than I'm used to. Being with Genevieve brings something out of me, a carnal hunger I can't ignore.

"I'm looking," she says, her voice even. "Fuck me, Finn."

I didn't think it was possible for me to get even more turned on.

I was wrong.

I tighten my hold on her hair, gripping her hip harder. Then I thrust in and out of her in a punishing pace.

"Come on, Gen. Get off on me," I grunt. "I don't know how much longer I can last."

"Then let go," she pants.

I vehemently shake my head. "You first."

"I don't know if I can. I—"

"You can. And you will." I release her hair, but she keeps her stare on me. I lick my finger, then I lower it to her clit, taking over for her and rubbing slow circles.

She pulses against me with increased desperation, as if encouraging me to keep going. I feel her walls tightening, her breathing growing even more ragged until she spasms around me, her cries of pleasure filling the room.

"Thank god," I exhale, clutching her hips hard now that she's gotten off. Then I drive into her relentlessly, feeling more like a wild animal than a human capable of compassion and empathy. None of that matters right now. All that does is chasing this unrelenting craving inside of me.

When she moans my name, I lose all control, a roar ripping from my throat as I spill into her. And it feels damn incredible to be able to do that. To feel her with nothing between us.

My orgasm seems to go on and on, wave after wave of bliss washing over me until I have nothing left. I slow my motions, continuing to move in and out of her until the last of our tremors have subsided.

Then I fold my body over hers, forcing her head to the side and capturing her mouth in a kiss. She doesn't deny me, even though my job is technically done for the night. She sighs into me, allowing me to savor this connection for a few more moments.

"I've never done that before," I say breathlessly.

"What do you mean?"

"Come inside another woman. I've always worn condoms."

She lets out a small laugh. "I'm glad I could be your first." Then her smile falters slightly, like she just realized how intimate that actually sounds. Clearing her throat, she adds, "Speaking of which, I should probably lie on my back. Not sure if it's true or not, but some say it helps increase your chances."

"Right. Of course." I ease out of her, noticing a subtle shiver roll through her. Supporting her, I help her onto her back, her hair fanning out over the pillow.

"You can use my shower if you want."

"Your shower?" I furrow my brows.

"So you don't have to leave here smelling like sex… Or me."

I should probably take her up on the offer. Should do whatever I can to draw some kind of line between what we just did and our friendship.

Instead, I shake my head and cage her in between my arms.

"Sweetheart, I plan on keeping your scent on me as long as possible."

I capture her lips with mine, kissing her slow and

deep, our tongues briefly tangling before I force myself to pull back.

And then, silence.

Not a comfortable one.

The kind that stretches, heavy and uncertain, making the air feel thick with all the things we're not saying.

I've never had trouble fucking a woman and walking away afterward. Never hesitated to pull on my clothes, make some polite excuse, and leave without looking back.

Why does the idea of leaving Genevieve right now sit wrong in my chest?

This is what we agreed to, though.

Just sex to get her pregnant. And when we're not having sex, we're just friends.

Nothing more.

"I'll let you get some sleep since you have to work tomorrow," I finally say, unsure what else to do now that we've done what we set out to do.

She parts her lips, then hesitates before saying, "Thanks."

Thanks.

I don't know why that word hits me wrong. As if I just fixed her sink or helped her move furniture.

As if I didn't just feel her lose all control with me.

"Of course," I manage, forcing an awkward smile as I yank my boxer briefs up my legs, then pull on my jeans.

By the time I tug my t-shirt over my head, she's already wrapped herself up in the duvet. Almost like she's hiding. Or creating space.

I remind myself I'll see her again tomorrow. *Feel* her again tomorrow.

Leaning down, I press a soft kiss to her forehead. "Sweet dreams, Genevieve."

She exhales, her eyes briefly closing. "'Night, Finn."

I linger a second longer, inhaling her scent. Then I force myself to leave.

THIRTEEN

Genevieve

I stare at the spreadsheet on my computer screen, willing myself to focus. Line items and numbers blur together, and I let out a frustrated sigh, rubbing my temple. No matter how hard I try, I can't keep my mind from drifting back to last night.

To Finn.

To the way he made me feel things I never thought possible.

I had no idea sex could be like that. Had no idea it could be that good.

Although I'm not sure good is an adequate enough word to describe what it felt like to be with Finn.

Incredible.

Amazing.

Life changing.

Sex with Ethan always felt…mechanical. Like I was just something else he was checking off his to-do list for the day.

Unload the dishwasher. Fold the laundry. Sleep with my wife.

But Finn… He touched me like he *needed* me. Like he couldn't go another second without feeling me. There was so much passion, so much intensity. I was completely unprepared for how easily he unraveled me.

And how much I craved him, even after he left.

I nearly asked him to stay. Rationalized it would give us more opportunities to have sex, increasing my chances of getting pregnant.

Thankfully, I quickly came to my senses.

It's one thing to have sex in order to get pregnant.

It's another to let him into my bed. Let him wrap his arms around me. Let myself pretend, even for a second, this is who we are to each other.

A sharp knock at my office door jolts me from my thoughts, and Claire waltzes in, practically vibrating with excitement as she drops into the chair across from me.

"How was it?"

I school my expression. "How was what?"

"Don't play dumb," she scoffs. "Last night. With Finn."

I shrug, forcing an air of indifference. "It was…fine."

She narrows her eyes. "*Fine*?"

"That's what I said."

I shift my focus to my computer, pretending to be extremely busy.

The numbers blur even more.

"Liar."

I glance at her. "I don't know what you want me to say."

"How about the truth?" She leans in, her eyes bright with mischief. "Was it amazing? Cathartic? Transcendental?"

"You sound like mom. It was just sex," I remind her.

"That may be what you're telling yourself, but I know you, Gen. And I know you try to downplay anything that affects you. Which is precisely why I get the feeling last night affected you. That it *wasn't* just sex."

I hesitate for a moment, about to reiterate my argument it *was* just sex. But this is my sister. We've had each other's back through all of life's ups and downs. After last night, I *really* need someone to talk to.

Someone who can help me make sense of this.

Claire may be six years younger than me, but she's always been my closest confidant… Besides Finn.

And this isn't something I can talk to him about.

"It was one of the best nights of my life," I blurt out.

"I knew it!" She claps her hands together and bounces excitedly in her chair, a wide grin on her face. "It's about damn time you got properly laid."

"Claire!" I hiss, pinning her with a glare. "Keep your voice down. You're in a library. The last thing I need is for my personal life to be broadcast all over town."

"Whatever." She rolls her eyes. "There's nothing wrong with having a healthy sex life."

"I don't have a sex life."

"Then what did you do last night with Finn? Crochet? Play bingo at the senior center? Clip coupons?"

"Actually, we went mini golfing."

She waggles her brows. "And he got a hole in one."

"What are you? Twelve?"

"I'm just happy for you." She reaches across the desk and covers my hand with hers. "You deserve this, especially after being married to boring Ethan Brody for all those years."

"He wasn't *that* boring."

Claire shoots me a disbelieving look. "Gen, he color-coded his closet. His idea of being spontaneous was ordering a different brand of toothpaste. Hell, he talked about spreadsheets with the same excitement I had when we got tickets to see Taylor Swift."

"He's an accountant. He likes numbers."

She arches a single brow, still not buying my argument.

"Maybe he was a *little* boring," I finally admit.

"A little?"

I roll my eyes but can't help the small laugh that escapes. She *does* have a point. Ethan didn't have a spontaneous bone in his body. But I didn't want spontaneous. I wanted reliable. Responsible.

That was Ethan.

"Maybe that's why you married him," Claire suggests after a protracted silence.

I frown, raising my mug to my lips, sipping on my now cold coffee. "What do you mean?"

"Ethan is everything Finn isn't. Safe. Predictable. Someone you knew you'd never love."

"What are you talking about? We were married."

"But did you love him?"

I start to respond, but she cuts me off.

"I'm not talking about the kind of love you have for me or Mom. I mean the kind of love that knocks the air from your lungs. The kind that makes you feel alive and terrified at the same time. The kind that would make you risk everything for just one more second with that person. Did you love Ethan like that?"

I don't immediately say anything. But I don't have to. Claire knows what my answer will be.

More importantly, so do I.

I never loved Ethan like that.

I may have *wanted* to love him that way. He checked all the boxes. He was steady, reliable, and wanted a family. More importantly, he didn't seem like the person who would abandon his commitment.

To me, that was more important than love.

I should have known it wouldn't be enough. That even if you choose the right person, the *perfect* person, they'll eventually leave. They always do.

"Love is overrated," I reply, ignoring her question. "That love you read about in your books and see on TV? It's *fiction*, Claire. An illusion sold to the masses. It's not real."

"It can be if you stopped closing yourself off to the idea of it. Don't you want more?"

"Why do you think I'm doing this? I'm trying to get pregnant so I can have a baby, for crying out loud. It may not be *your* version of living a full, complete life, but it is for me. I've always wanted a family. I'm willing to do whatever is necessary so I can have that. That's what's important to me at this point in my life."

She gives me a skeptical look then finally pushes out a long sigh. "If you say so."

"I do. This is what I want," I reiterate, squaring my shoulders. "Just a baby. Nothing more."

But despite my insistence, a niggle of doubt has already taken root inside me. It's been there since last night.

I fear it'll only grow stronger the more Finn and I blur the lines of our friendship.

FOURTEEN

Finn

I draw in a deep breath as I make my way up to Genevieve's house, my stomach coiled tight with something I'm not used to around her.

Nerves?

No. That's ridiculous. This is Genevieve. My best friend. The woman I've known since we were kids.

And I'm here to try to get her pregnant. No big deal. It's fine. *We're* fine.

But despite all our reassurances that things wouldn't change, something in my gut tells me we've already crossed a line we can't uncross.

Because last night wasn't just sex.

I want to call it that, but it doesn't sit right. Not when I spent all day thinking about it. Thinking about *her*.

I can still feel the heat of her body under mine. Can still hear her voice as she gasped my name. Can still taste her pussy on my tongue.

No. Regardless of what I want to tell myself, last night was so much more than sex.

As I approach Genevieve's front door, I reach for the keypad, but hesitate.

Should I knock instead?

I've let myself in more times than I can count. Why should it be different now?

She made it clear. This isn't supposed to change us. We're friends first and always. And maybe if I start acting like I usually do around her, I'll stop feeling this way.

Resolved, I punch in my code and step inside.

"Genevieve?" I call out when I don't see her in the open living area. "It's me."

She pokes her head around the kitchen corner, a bright smile lighting up her face. It's the same greeting I've grown accustomed to throughout our friendship. Nothing different. Nothing awkward.

"I'm just finishing up dinner."

My stomach rumbles at the smell of onions and peppers, and I follow the scent into the kitchen. "It already smells great."

"Want a beer?" she asks, expertly rolling a tortilla stuffed with vegetables and black beans.

"I can get it." I pop open the fridge and grab a

bottle containing the familiar logo of Jude's brewery before facing her again. "Need any help?"

"Just need to get these in the oven." She spreads sauce over the enchiladas before layering on cheese, her movements practiced and easy. After sliding the dish into the oven, she sets the timer and turns to me, wiping her hands on a towel. "They'll be ready in twenty minutes."

"Want to watch an episode of *Schitt's Creek*?"

It's what we usually do whenever I come over for dinner.

Which is often, since I'm not the best cook and Genevieve loves it. It's a win-win.

"Actually…" She closes the distance between us, her gaze hooded, her body language shifting in a way that makes my pulse spike. "I thought we could do something else while we wait."

"What's that?" I ask, my voice rough.

She hoists herself onto her toes. Her warm breath drifts along my neck, making my cock immediately harden.

"Instead of telling you, why don't I show you?"

I've always thought Genevieve was sexy. You'd have to be blind not to. Long legs. Incredible curves. Lips I've fantasized about more times than I care to admit.

But hearing her whisper in that husky voice nearly undoes me.

She lowers herself back to her heels, then turns,

slowly making her way out of the kitchen and down the hallway.

I don't immediately move, taking a moment to enjoy the sight of her hips swaying as she walks.

"We're down to eighteen minutes, Finn," she calls out over her shoulder.

She doesn't have to tell me twice.

I hastily set my bottle onto the counter and take off after her, ripping my t-shirt over my head as I go.

The second I enter the bedroom, she throws her arms around me, crushing her lips against mine.

I spent all day trying to shake this feeling, but the second her tongue tangles with mine, it's clear I never stood a chance. I dig my fingers into her hair, holding her close, a raw desperation taking over.

She tears away, kissing a path down my jaw, nipping at my throat, and it's like she's set out to ruin me.

Something about her is different tonight. She's not timid or reserved, not like she was last night, at least in the beginning. Tonight, she's a woman who exudes confidence. Who knows what she wants.

And right now, that's me.

"There's something I want to do," she announces, locking her eyes with mine. "It's something I've always wanted to try, but anytime I suggested it to Ethan, he sort of turned me down. But I want to try it with you, if you're okay with it."

I cup her cheek, inching my mouth toward hers

and brushing a soft kiss to her lips. "I know the purpose of this is for you to get pregnant, but there's nothing wrong with killing two birds with one stone, so to speak. I'm more than happy to help you explore your fantasies. You're safe with me."

"Thank you." She presses her mouth more firmly against mine, coaxing my lips to part, her tongue swiping with mine in a too brief dance before she pulls back.

"What did you have in mind? Blindfold? Being tied up? Spanking? Breath play? What is it?"

"Nothing like that." She tries to avert her gaze, but I won't let her.

"Don't get all shy on me now. Tell me what you want."

She hesitates for a beat. Then she says, "I've always wanted to give a guy a blow job."

I go completely still.

My pulse kicks into overdrive, my body tensing as my brain scrambles to process what she just said.

"Forget it." She shifts, suddenly looking self-conscious. "We can just—"

I grip her wrist, pulling her back against me. "Are you telling me Ethan never wanted you to suck his cock?"

She swallows hard. "He said it never appealed to him."

I look at her in complete shock. I never liked Ethan. Never thought he was good enough for

Genevieve, but he seemed to make her happy, so I kept my mouth shut.

But the more she shares about him, the more I realize what a fucking tool he really is.

"He's a goddamn idiot, Genevieve."

A blush rises on her cheeks, but I don't miss the way her pupils dilate, the way her breath hitches.

"We don't have to. I don't want you to feel like—"

I cut her off with a slow, deep kiss, then pull back just enough to murmur against her lips. "Stop sacrificing your needs for someone else."

She shivers against me, a barely audible whimper escaping her throat.

"I've been fantasizing what you'd look like with your lips wrapped around my cock for longer than I'd like to admit. So get on your knees."

She stares at me, her mouth parting slightly, hesitation flickering across her face.

For a second, I wonder if I pushed too hard.

Then she leans in and brushes her lips along my throat.

"Yes, sir."

I squeeze my eyes shut.

As if it isn't enough of a turn on to know my dick will be the first she's ever had in her mouth, hearing those words in her sultry voice is almost too much.

Almost.

She leaves rough kisses along my neck and torso, the combination of her tongue circling and teeth nipping driving me fucking crazy as she slowly lowers herself to her knees.

When she reaches for my jeans, she floats her gaze back to mine.

"Take me out," I tell her, sensing she needs me to take charge. Tell her what to do. Let her know I'm okay with this.

Hell, I'm *more* than okay with this.

This has been my adolescent fantasy for what feels like forever.

As she unbuttons my jeans and lowers the zipper, it feels like time stands still. I hold my breath, my pulse thundering in my ears. Finally she pushes my briefs down and my erection springs free.

"You're so hard."

I release a small laugh. "You tell me you want to suck my cock and you don't think I'd instantly get hard?"

She doesn't immediately say anything. Just shrugs.

We never went into details about her relationship with Ethan, despite our years-long friendship. Now that we are, I get the feeling Ethan never made her feel cherished. Admired.

Wanted.

That's exactly what I plan to do over the next few days.

"You're fucking incredible, Genevieve," I say as I grip her cheek. "All day, it's taken every ounce of resolve I possess not to jerk off at the memory of being with you last night. Now let me feel your mouth on me."

She slowly shifts her gaze back to mine, her breaths growing ragged. Then she licks her lips and wraps her hand around my erection.

"Fuck," I hiss, squeezing my eyes shut. If this is how I react when her mouth isn't even on me, I have no idea how I'm going to last. But I'll do my best so she can have this. So she can explore her fantasies.

She gives me a few slow, gentle tugs, although I doubt I could get any harder. When she drags her tongue along her lips again, I'm ready to lose my mind. I've never wanted something as much as I want my cock in Genevieve's mouth.

I'm about to tell her so when she finally brings her lips up to me, her tongue teasing me with a few torturous circles.

"Goddamn," I groan, moving my hand to her hair and gripping it hard, needing something to keep me grounded.

She drags her tongue down one side before teasing my tip again. I brace myself for her to take me completely in her mouth. Being the tease she is, she then licks her way down the other side of my cock.

"Genevieve, if you don't put my dick in your mouth right now, I'm going to lose it."

"Impatient, much?" She smirks, giving me a playful look.

"When it comes to you, you better fucking believe it."

"Well, then, I wouldn't want to keep you waiting."

She licks her lips again, slowly inching back to me. When she takes me in her mouth, I have to fight the urge to thrust into her, the need to bury my dick deep in her throat overwhelming. But she's never done this before. I need to start her out easy.

"So fucking good," I tell her, keeping my hold on her head firm. "Your mouth feels so damn good."

She hums her response, the vibration against my dick driving me fucking crazy.

"You should see how beautiful you look with your mouth full of my cock."

She moans again, continuing to bob up and down.

"That turns you on, doesn't it? It turns you on having my dick filling your mouth?"

Her agreement shows in her increased enthusiasm as she continues to torture me. I hold her head with both of my hands, gently thrusting in and out of her.

She whimpers, and I pause.

"Too much?" I arch a brow.

She pulls her mouth off me for a beat. "Not enough. Go harder. Deeper."

"Are you sure?"

"I told you last night. I want to know what it can be like. I don't want you to be gentle with me, Finn. I like exploring these things with you. Don't hold back because you don't think I can handle it." She levels me with a determined stare, not a single ounce of hesitation within. "I want you to use my mouth."

I'm surprised I don't come right then and there. Those are words I never thought I'd hear my best friend say, especially to me. But I can't ignore the pride that swells inside me over the idea that she's comfortable enough with me to give voice to her deepest fantasies.

Wrapping my hand around my dick, I bring the tip up to her mouth. "Open," I order.

She obediently complies, parting her lips, practically salivating for me.

"Wrap your lips around me," I tell her.

Again, she does as I ask, slowly taking me in her mouth, her tongue licking and torturing me as she does.

I grip both sides of her head, forcing her to take more and more of me. She doesn't resist. Instead, she closes her eyes and moans, squirming slightly.

"You want me to use this mouth?"

She looks at me and gives a subtle nod.

"Good. Now loosen that jaw and let me all the way in."

I feel her muscles relax as I ease further in, every inch I push making my breathing increase. When I hit the back of her throat, she whimpers, closing her eyes.

"Look at me. I want your eyes on me when I fuck your mouth."

She snaps her gaze back to mine, her eyes watering, tears staining her cheeks. But she doesn't retreat. Still keeps her stare trained on mine with my cock buried deep inside her throat, something inside telling me she wants even more.

I tighten my grip on her head and retreat before thrusting back inside, my motions intensifying with every punishing drive. Each one only seems to turn Genevieve on more, her moans and whimpers increasing with desperation. I'm on the brink of losing control, but I don't want this to be over yet. This very well could be the one and only time Genevieve ever gives me a blow job. I want it to last as long as possible.

My dick doesn't seem to get the message, though. Even when I slow my rhythm, Genevieve continues torturing me with her mouth and tongue.

"Shit, Gen. I'm close."

I try to pull out of her, but she grips my ass, forcing my erection back into her mouth.

I figured she'd suck my dick, but once I was close, she'd want me to come inside her. After all, the only reason for any of this is to for her to get pregnant.

But that seems to be the last thing on her mind right now.

She moves against my length with more enthusiasm. When she cups my balls, I can't control it anymore. I explode in her mouth, her tongue lapping up every last drop until I have nothing left, my muscles going slack.

She comes off me with a sheepish smile. "I guess I got a little carried away."

I yank her to her feet, pulling her body flush with mine. "You can suck my cock anytime you want."

"Was it okay?"

"Okay?" I shoot back incredulously. "It was… It was fucking amazing, Genevieve." I crash my mouth to hers, tasting me and her in one intoxicating combination.

But before I can deepen the kiss, the oven buzzes and she pushes against me.

"To be continued." She flashes me a wink, then turns, her hips swaying as she makes her way down the hallway.

FIFTEEN

Genevieve

I do my best to pretend my body isn't still buzzing, even nearly a half-hour later, while Finn and I sit on the couch, watching *Schitt's Creek* as we eat the dinner I'd prepared for us — veggie and black bean enchiladas and Spanish rice.

I didn't plan on giving him a blow job when he first arrived. I figured we could use the twenty minutes it took for the food to cook to have sex, if for no other reason than to remind myself why we're doing this. That it's just sex. A means to an end.

But my plan backfired spectacularly.

I still don't know what came over me. All I know is that being with Finn feels different. *Safer*. As if I don't have to hide from him. The way he touches me, the way he looks at me, it makes me feel seen in a way I never have before.

Whenever I asked Ethan to try certain things, he made me feel like I was wrong for wanting them. Like there was something broken in me for needing more than the bare minimum.

I convinced myself it was okay. I could take care of my needs on my own.

But Finn allows me to explore my desires. Hell, he *encourages* it. There are no feelings of shame or inadequacy. No having to shrink myself to make someone else comfortable. Only raw hunger.

A part of me thinks I should put a stop to all this foreplay. That I should take a page out of Ethan's book and insist Finn and I stick to mechanical, emotionless sex. Make it clinical. Impersonal.

But I get the feeling that's impossible with us. We have too strong of a connection. Too much history. Too much…chemistry.

"Are you done?" Finn's deep voice yanks me out of my thoughts, and I snap my gaze toward him.

Apparently, I'd been so lost in my head he thinks I'm finished eating, even though I barely touched my food.

But I'm not all that hungry.

"Yeah."

"Are you okay?" He eyes my plate.

"I had a late lunch," I lie, standing from the couch and picking up my dish.

"I got it," he says, taking it from me.

I murmur my thanks and follow him into the kitchen, where we settle into our usual routine of cleaning up after dinner. He rinses the dishes before placing them into the dishwasher while I clean up the leftovers and put them in the refrigerator.

It's a routine we've done hundreds of times. Tonight, though, there's an electricity in the room that hasn't been here any other time.

Every brush of his fingers as I pass him a plate, every slight lean of his body when he reaches for something near me, sends shivers over my skin. I tell myself it's just residual tension from earlier. That Finn could be anyone and I'd be acting like this.

But I know it's a lie.

"Let me squeeze by," Finn murmurs, his voice lower now. Rougher.

His hand lands on my hip as he leans into me, reaching for the cabinet overhead and setting a wine glass inside. His chest is warm and solid against my back, his breath feathering over my neck.

A soft sound escapes before I can swallow it down, especially when his groin brushes against my ass. He's not even hard, but my libido doesn't seem to care. She's ready to go, desperate to experience the bliss only Finn's been able to pull out of me.

"Everything okay, Genevieve?" he asks, amusement dripping from his voice.

"Uh, huh. Great." My response comes out uneven, my pitch higher than usual.

He steps back, but when I glance over my shoulder, his eyes trace over my every movement.

"You sure about that?" Arms crossed, he leans against the island, a slow smirk stretching his lips.

"Absolutely." I grab the cleaner and spray some onto the counter, wiping down the surface, even though I distinctly remember him doing the same thing seconds ago.

It gives me something to do. Something to focus on that isn't him. That isn't the heat simmering in my veins, making it harder and harder to pretend this is nothing more than a convenient arrangement.

But Finn doesn't let me pretend for long.

I feel him approach before I hear him, his body radiating heat as he reaches for my wrist and takes the dish towel from me.

"You seem tense." His breath grazes my ear.

It takes everything in me to stay upright, my knees threatening to give out.

"I'm fine," I barely squeak out.

"Then perhaps I can interest you in some dessert."

"I… I'm not sure what I have." I swallow hard.

He chuckles, the low vibration hitting me in places I didn't know existed. "We both know there's only one kind of dessert I'm interested in."

Before I can react, he spins me to face him, his

hands gripping my hips, his body pressing me against the counter. The moment his mouth crashes into mine, any illusion of control disintegrates.

Finn kisses me like he's starving. Like I'm the only thing that can ever satisfy his hunger. And I want to believe it's real. I want to believe it so badly it scares me.

In one swift move, he shoves my yoga pants down my legs and lifts me onto the counter I just cleaned.

When he tears his lips from mine, I ask, "What are you doing?"

His grin is pure sin, the kind that always precedes him doing something dangerous.

"Having dessert."

Then he drops to his knees, pulling me to the edge of the island. His tongue swipes along my center, his fingers inching inside me, and I can't think anymore. Can't breathe. Can't do anything but feel.

"God, I love dessert," I moan, fisting my hands in his hair.

"Me, too, Genevieve," he rasps, briefly meeting my gaze before returning his attention to me. "I love *your* dessert. I'm so damn addicted to it. Can eat it every day and still not get my fill."

I squeeze my eyes shut, willing myself not to fall for his words. He's just saying what he thinks I want to hear. Just playing the part of a man who can't get enough of me.

That's all this is.

A fantasy.

Nothing more.

In a few days, we'll go back to normal. Pretend this never happened.

And I'll pretend it didn't break me to let him go.

SIXTEEN

Finn

Smoke curls from the grill, wrapping the air in the scent of charred meat and smoldering charcoal. Jude flips burgers with exaggerated precision, his brows drawn in tight focus, while my other brother, Beckham, stands beside him, shaking his head like he's witnessing a crime.

"Damn shame," Beckham mutters, crossing his tattooed arms.

Jude glares at him. "What?"

"You're murdering those burgers."

Jude scoffs, flipping another patty. "You always talk shit, but remind me…" He shifts to face Beckham, pointing at the apron tied around his waist. "What does this say again?"

Beckham rolls his eyes as he takes a sip from his beer.

It's odd to see him drinking anything other than wine, considering he owns one of the most successful vineyards in the area. But some days just call for beer, and today is one of those days. The kind where the sun hangs warm and steady in a blue-washed sky. The kind that tastes like summer.

"Anyone can buy an apron that says *King of the Grill*. Doesn't mean you're any good at it."

Mom groans as she strolls past us, placing a bowl of salad on the table. "For heaven's sake, you two are grown men. Can we go one family gathering without arguing over who's a better cook?"

"No," my brothers say in unison.

"I hate to break it to you, but neither of you are the best cook in the family," she retorts. "That title belongs to Dylan." She gives them a smile, then heads back into the house, probably to get even more food.

It doesn't matter how many times we tell her not to go overboard for Sunday dinner.

She won't hear it.

Either will Dylan.

"Only because she went to culinary school," Jude mutters under his breath. "I'm pretty good for an amateur."

"You're an amateur, all right," Beckham retorts, which earns him a flip of the middle finger from Jude.

"What's worse?" I nudge my oldest brother,

Hayden, who stands beside me on the patio, his arms loosely crossed. "The way they bicker, or the fact that Mom still thinks she can stop them?"

"Both." His laugh is quiet, but it's there. After everything he's been through, after losing his wife, I'll take it. There was a time I didn't think I'd see him smile again.

Some days are harder than others, but he's healing. Slowly.

"They're worse than my kids."

As if summoned, his daughter, Presley, and Beckham's stepdaughter, Maggie, come bouncing up, stopping in front of the grill. Well, Maggie bounces. Presley stands quietly beside her, hands folded in front of her.

Maggie flips her auburn curls over her shoulder and fixes Beckham with her most persuasive look. "Beck, we have a very important request," she says with a slight lisp from where she recently lost a tooth.

He eyes her warily. "And what's that?"

She puffs out her tiny chest. "We would like to make s'mores early."

"That so?" Hayden arches a brow, taking a slow sip of his beer.

Presley nods solemnly.

"We've discussed it," Maggie says.

I don't even question how this is possible when Presley hasn't spoken a word since the accident that took her mother.

Over the past several months since Beckham married Haley, Maggie's mother, I've seen how close Presley and Maggie have become, even though Presley's two years older. Whenever they're together, Presley seems genuinely happy. And Maggie doesn't pressure her to talk like some of the other kids at school do. It's as if they have their own way of communicating. Maggie's been the best thing for Presley.

And for Beckham, too.

"We already know we want s'mores," Maggie continues. "So why not just eat them now?"

Beckham and Hayden exchange a look.

"That *is* compelling logic," Hayden offers.

"True," Beckham agrees, stroking his stubbled jaw as if seriously considering the request. "But who's going to tell your mom you filled up on sugar before dinner?"

Maggie's confidence falters. "Um…you?"

Beckham chuckles. "Nice try, kiddo." He ruffles her curls. "But dinner first. *Then* dessert."

With dramatic defeat, Maggie sighs. "Fine. We'll wait. But only if you play pirate ship with us." Her little eyes light up.

Hayden exhales as he brings his beer to his mouth, finishing it before tossing the bottle into the bin. "Guess it's pirate time, Beckham."

"Argh," Beckham deadpans, following the girls

toward the giant playscape that resembles a pirate ship.

As I watch them walk toward the play area, my gaze drifts unbidden to someone else.

Genevieve sits in the grass, playing with Hayden's son, Jeremiah. Sunlight spills over her hair, catching the warm, rich tones. Jeremiah hands her a toy truck, babbling in that animated way only a toddler can, and she nods along, like whatever he's saying is the most fascinating thing in the world.

She's always been good with kids, but seeing her like this, so natural and at ease with Jeremiah, solidifies what I already knew.

Genevieve deserves this. Deserves to be a mother.

"So, you brought Genevieve to Sunday dinner," Jude remarks after a beat, dragging my focus away.

I take a sip of my beer, feigning nonchalance. "And? She's my friend. Need I remind you that you invited Abbey when you were supposedly 'just roommates'?"

Jude's mouth twitches as he glances at the tall blonde sitting with Genevieve and Haley.

While Abbey started out as a runaway bride in need of a job and a place to live, both of which Jude gave her, she's now much more than a roommate or employee to him, something we all saw from the beginning but he refused to admit.

Until we talked some sense into him.

"Technically, Mom invited Abbey the first time."

"And the second?"

His smile broadens. "The second was all me."

"Thought so." I take another sip of my beer, trying to avoid looking at Genevieve, but it's impossible. Whenever she's around, I'm drawn to her.

"So there's no *other* reason she's here?" Jude presses, lowering his voice. "Something relating to our last conversation?"

I hesitate, not immediately answering. What do I say? Genevieve made it clear she wanted to keep my role in her potential pregnancy quiet. But Jude already knows I was thinking about offering to help.

"Maybe."

His eyebrows lift. "Does that mean you two are… you know?"

I give a subtle nod.

Jude stares at me for a beat, then grins. "I knew it was only a matter of time."

"What was only a matter of time?" Dylan asks, approaching with a platter of vegetables on skewers and setting them down on the table beside the grill.

Jude and I share a look, neither of us saying anything. And Jude won't. He'll keep it quiet if that's what I want.

"Are you talking about you and Genevieve?" she presses when I remain silent.

"What do you mean?"

My sister snorts. "Oh, come on. You've been staring

at her all afternoon. And she's been staring right back." She pinches her lips together as a contemplative expression crosses her face. "I could be misreading things, but there's something…different between you two today."

I should shut this down. Make a joke. Change the subject. But now that I'm in unfamiliar territory with my best friend, I could use someone to talk to who won't give me shit.

I glance at Jude, who simply shrugs, telling me to do what I think is best. Then I refocus my attention on Dylan. She may be the baby of the family, but she's always been the thoughtful and introspective one. Maybe because she's the youngest of five and the only girl. Still, she always comes to things with a different perspective.

Right now, I could use that.

"Genevieve wants a baby," I tell her. "I agreed to help."

Dylan doesn't react the way I expect. There's no shock. No judgment. Just quiet curiosity as she walks to the cooler and grabs a beer, popping the top off.

After taking a long sip, she smooths a few blonde waves behind her ear, then asks, "When you say she wants a baby, is she hoping to adopt or—"

"She's trying to get pregnant naturally without medical intervention."

"And you're…helping her conceive."

"I am."

She hums, looking into the distance for a beat. "And when she gets pregnant?"

"Things go back to normal." I take a sip of my beer, but it tastes wrong now.

"What would be your responsibility at that point?"

"Nothing."

"Nothing?" she repeats.

"It's how Genevieve wants it. She wants a baby without having any sort of relationship with the father. She doesn't plan on telling anyone who the father is."

"And you're okay with being in her life, being in her *kid's* life, all the while knowing you're the father but won't be allowed to fulfill that role?"

"It's what she wants," I reiterate.

Jude sets a few of the vegetable skewers on the grill, then looks my way. "But what do *you* want?" he asks in a low voice.

"It doesn't matter."

"Of course it does," Dylan insists.

"I knew what I was getting into before we started down this path. I'm fine with it. In fact, I'm thrilled she trusts me enough to be a part of it. She deserves this."

"Is that the *only* reason?" She crosses a single arm over her stomach

"What other reason is there? I'm her friend. This is what friends do."

She narrows her gaze on me. "I could be wrong,

but this sort of thing goes far beyond the bounds of friendship." Pausing, she takes a deliberate sip of her beer as she rakes her analytical eyes over me. "You have feelings for her."

"What?" I shoot back quickly, glancing at Jude for support, but only find a knowing grin. "I mean, I *care* about her. As a friend."

Even I can't ignore the sour taste in my mouth as the words leave me.

"Because you never considered there could be more," Jude offers.

"You're being ridiculous." I take a long pull from my beer, purposefully avoiding their stares.

"You've always kept Genevieve in this little box labeled 'best friend,' because you never let yourself entertain the *possibility* of anything else," Dylan states very matter-of-factly.

"Genevieve isn't looking for love," I deflect. "It's why she's chosen this path."

"She doesn't want *heartbreak*," Jude interjects quickly. "Trust me. There's a difference."

If anyone would know, it's Jude. He did the same thing. It's why he almost lost Abbey. But before I can come up with a detailed list of why my situation is different, Genevieve's laughter rings out, pulling my attention to her.

She's still playing with Jeremiah, her smile bright and carefree.

And damn if it doesn't hit me right in the chest all over again.

"You want my opinion?" Dylan's voice drags me back to her.

"I'm pretty sure you're going to give it whether I want it or not."

"True." She flashes a sly grin. "For as long as I can remember, you've been there for Gen. You're always ready and willing to drop everything for her when she needs it. Even when she doesn't. You *always* show up for her."

"Because she's my friend," I reiterate my argument.

"So is Murphy. Do you show up like that for him?"

I part my lips to say yes, but the answer won't come.

Because my sister has a point.

I show up like this for Genevieve because of *who* she is.

"You've been stepping up for her for a long time, Finn," Dylan continues, her voice softer now. "Maybe you should finally ask yourself why."

I swallow hard, gripping my beer.

Then I shake my head.

"She's just a friend," I repeat, refusing to go there.

I can't.

Not with everything I stand to lose by even entertaining the idea of something more.

SEVENTEEN

Finn

The drive back to Genevieve's house is quiet. Not the comfortable kind of silence we're used to, but the thick, suffocating kind that presses against my ribs.

Genevieve stares out the passenger window, her fingers absently tracing a pattern on the door handle. I grip the steering wheel tighter, unable to stop thinking about what my sister said.

Is there another reason I go above and beyond for Genevieve?

Of course, I care about her. She's my best friend. She *has* been since we were in diapers.

But is there more to it? Is there a deeper reason I always go out of my way for Genevieve?

Damn Dylan and her stupid remarks.

Why does she seem to know exactly what to say to make me second-guess everything?

I pull into Genevieve's driveway and shift my truck into park. Neither of us moves right away. It's like we both know once we step out, we'll face an ending we can't prevent.

If she gets pregnant, this arrangement is over. We go back to being friends, nothing more.

I should be okay with that.

Then why does every cell in my body feel like it's revolting against the prospect of tonight being the last time I ever feel her?

Genevieve's the first to move, unbuckling her seatbelt and sliding out. I follow, my feet heavier with each step toward her front door. We both remain silent as she lets us inside, locking the door behind her before heading down the hallway.

And again, I follow.

When we reach the bedroom, she turns to face me. The low light catches the uncertainty in her gray eyes, amplifying the tension in my chest and making it ache all over again.

"Last night," she murmurs.

I'm not sure if it's for her benefit or mine.

I nod, my throat thick. "Last night."

Then we lunge for each other.

Her mouth crashes against mine, our bodies moving with a desperation that feels like finality.

There's no hesitation. No slow build-up. Just raw, unrestrained need.

Her fingers tear at my shirt, and my hands slide beneath the hem of hers, brushing warm skin as I pull it over her head. There's no careful restraint. No keeping my distance, even emotionally.

I let myself *have* her.

Because after this, I may never have her again.

We strip each other bare, and when I lower her onto the bed, I force myself to slow down. To *savor*. I settle between her legs, holding her gaze as I push inside her, drinking in every flicker of pleasure on her expression.

I lace my fingers through hers, anchoring myself in the moment. She doesn't push me to go faster, and I don't rush. We stay like this, moving in sync, stretching every second, like we both know this might be the last time.

And I hate the thought.

But I knew what I was getting into. Get her pregnant, and we go back to being friends.

Can I go back to being friends, though?

"Hold on, beautiful," I croon when I feel her tighten around me.

We've only been intimate for mere days, but in that short time I've learned to read her body. Know where she needs me to touch her. Know when she needs it faster. And I know when she's about to lose all control.

Like right now.

I lower my lips toward hers. "I want to come with you."

"I don't know if I can hold on much longer." Her legs tighten around my waist, her voice breaking. "You feel too good."

When she drags her nails down my spine, I lose what little control I've managed to hold on to, her touch propelling me higher and higher.

I pulse into her, increasing my rhythm as I chase the feeling of bliss I've only experienced with her. Her breaths become ragged and uneven, and I drive into her with more desperation. Finally, she releases a strangled cry, her walls spasming around me at the same time as I jerk through my release, crashing my lips to hers in what I fear will be the last time I ever kiss her.

Even when I have nothing left, I don't stop kissing her.

And she doesn't push me away.

Instead, she clings to me, her hands ghosting over my skin as if she's memorizing what I feel like. Like she doesn't want this to end any more than I do.

But it has to.

Because the longer I stay here, the harder it will be to walk away.

The more I'll want something I have no business wanting.

I reluctantly bring our kiss to an end, and pull

back, searching her face for something. A reason to stay. A reason to pretend this isn't the end.

She parts her lips like she's going to say something, then shakes her head and forces a smile. "I'll let you know if it worked and we can determine next month's schedule if needed."

The words knock the wind out of me. They're clinical. Detached.

Like this was nothing more than a means to an end.

Which is exactly what it is.

"Sounds good." My response tastes bitter as I push myself up and reach for my clothes, dressing in silence.

At the door, I glance back at her, her eyes shadowed with something I can't quite name.

Then I turn and walk away before I make the mistake of doing something that might destroy our friendship more than my offer to knock her up in the first place.

EIGHTEEN

Genevieve

The sun filters through the trees as Claire and I walk along the winding path of the town park, the gravel crunching beneath our shoes. The summer air is warm, but I barely feel it. My mind is elsewhere, focused on the fact that my period was supposed to start yesterday. Sometimes I'm a day or two late, but I can't ignore the flutter of hope rising in my chest. The thought of a little life growing inside me sends a warmth through me.

And not just at the prospect of being pregnant, but at the idea of carrying Finn's child.

I quickly push down the thought. It's not his child.

It's *my* child.

This isn't about Finn.

It's about me having a family.

Finn's just the means of achieving that. Nothing more.

No emotions. No attachments. No promises.

Despite that, I'd be lying if I said I haven't missed the warmth of his hands on me. The way he kissed me. The quiet moments in the dark when I let myself pretend, just for a second, this was real.

But it's not real. It can't be. We agreed. After the way things ended with Ethan, a relationship is the last thing I want. I'm fine on my own. I'm *happy* on my own.

That still doesn't stop me from wondering what it might be like, especially after having a taste.

"How's Finn doing?" Claire's voice breaks through my thoughts, as if she's able to sense what I'm thinking about.

Considering how close we are, I wouldn't doubt it.

"Fine." I shrug, keeping my gaze fixed on the path ahead.

She narrows her eyes. "Fine? That's all you're going to give me after spending an entire week having what you described as the best sex of your life?"

"What do you want me to tell you, Claire? We had sex for a week, per an agreement we made in order for me to get pregnant. Per that agreement, after my ovulation window, things would return to normal, which they have."

While I wasn't sure if that would be possible, Finn's made sure things haven't been awkward between us. The day after the last time we had sex, he showed up at the library with coffee, like he often did before. There was no heat in his stare. No lingering glances. Just Finn, my friend. As if we never crossed that line.

As if I don't know how much pleasure he's capable of giving me.

"So you two just quit cold turkey?"

"We didn't *quit* anything. This is what we agreed to." I hold my head high, hoping she can't see the truth in my expression.

That I've missed having Finn in my bed.

That my vibrator's been getting quite the workout over the past ten days.

That when I close my eyes, I imagine it's Finn making me feel good. That it's his name on my lips whenever I make myself come.

"And you're okay with that?" Claire asks.

"That was the agreement," I remind her yet again.

"As you've said. Repeatedly." She gives me a pointed stare. "But forget the agreement for a second. Do you want more with him?"

"I *can't* want more with him." My candid response leaves my mouth before I can stop it.

"Because you have an agreement?" She arches a perfectly manicured brow. "Or because of Dad?"

I falter in my steps, darting my wide eyes toward her, her question leaving me momentarily speechless.

"He has nothing to do with this," I finally stammer out.

She exhales slowly and touches a soft hand to my arm, her green eyes awash with all the sincerity I've come to expect from my sister.

"Gen, I know what he did hurt you. I didn't really feel it since I never knew what it was like to have a father. But you can't keep letting his choices control your life."

"I'm not letting him control anything." I spin from her, kicking up dirt as I continue on the path.

"Aren't you?" she presses, easily catching up to me. "You're making decisions based on proving you don't need anyone. That you're fine on your own."

"Because I am," I snap back harsher than I intended, feeling the old wounds pressing in.

I was six when my dad walked out.

One day, he was kissing my forehead goodnight after reading me a bedtime story.

The next, his side of the closet was empty, and Mom was trying to smile through the tears, promising we'd be okay as she rubbed her very pregnant belly.

For months, I'd sit on the front steps waiting for his car to turn down the street. I went out of my way to be the perfect child. I thought if I was good enough, if I was quiet enough, he'd no longer feel like having kids was a mistake and would come back.

He never did.

I refuse to put my child through that.

Refuse to put *myself* through that.

"I don't want to depend on someone who could just walk away when things get hard," I declare.

"Not everyone leaves, Gen," Claire reminds me, studying me for a long moment. Then she pushes out a long sigh as she reaches into her pocket and retrieves her phone, scrolling through it before handing it to me.

I frown at the photo of Ethan and me from our wedding day. "Speaking of people who leave," I mutter under my breath.

"Tell me what you see," she challenges.

"I don't understand what this has to do with anything. I—"

"Stop being so damn stubborn and answer the question, Gen."

I exhale deeply, but play along. "I see myself dancing with the man I thought I wanted to spend my life with."

"How is he looking at you?"

I glance at Ethan's face. His posture is rigid, his gaze distant, almost indifferent. His expression isn't one of love or joy, but of obligation. Like he's simply enduring the moment rather than reveling in it. There's no warmth in his eyes, no tenderness in the way he holds me.

"Like he can't wait for the dance to be over."

Claire tilts her head. "And you?"

I study my own expression. My smile is tight,

forced. My shoulders are stiff, my body leaning ever so slightly away from Ethan rather than into him. I don't look happy. I don't even look content. If anything, I look uncomfortable. Like I already knew, deep down, I'd made a mistake.

"About the same."

Claire nods knowingly and takes her phone back. She swipes again before returning it to me. "Tell me what you see now."

It's another picture from my wedding. But this time, I'm dancing with Finn. And the way he's looking at me… God. It's not just different from Ethan. It's dangerous. Because as I look at that photo, I almost believe it.

That someone could look at me like I'm the best thing that ever happened to them.

Like they'll never walk away.

"This doesn't mean anything." I shove the phone back at my sister.

"I think it does. And I think you know it too, but you're too much of a coward to admit it."

I press my lips together, willing away the emotions tightening my throat.

Claire steps closer, placing a gentle hand on my arm. "Dad left because he was a fucking asshole who, one day, decided he no longer wanted the responsibility of having kids. What he did was shitty, but not everyone's like him. If you keep living your life like everyone is, you run the risk of missing out on so much."

Her words hit something raw inside me, scraping over wounds that never really healed.

Missing out.

Like Mom did? Loving a man who abandoned her, spending years picking up the pieces while he started fresh somewhere else, pretending we never existed?

I'd rather be alone than put myself through that.

"I'm not missing out on anything," I say, my voice cold, final.

Claire pins me with a glare, then just shakes her head, pushing out a resigned sigh. "If you say so."

NINETEEN

Finn

I go through the motions of checking my gear, adjusting my bunker pants, inspecting the regulator, but my thoughts keep drifting to Genevieve.

And the pregnancy test she planned to take this morning.

Is it negative, and she needs time to process the result before she shares the news with me?

Or is it positive, and she wants to tell me in person instead of over text?

A mixture of emotions grips me, excitement tangled with something bittersweet. I should be happy over the possibility she might be pregnant.

And I am.

But it also means I'll never get to touch her like that again. Never feel her body pressing into mine.

Never growl as her nails dig into my skin. Never hear that soft little gasp she makes when I first slide inside her.

I clench my jaw and squeeze my eyes shut, trying to think of something other than Genevieve, just as soft footsteps echo through the bay.

I snap my head up, a warmth filling me at the sight of Genevieve standing in the open bay doors. She's dressed in a pair of jeans and a t-shirt that says "A book worth banning is a book worth reading". I definitely don't remember a librarian ever looking this hot when I was growing up. Maybe if they were, I would have spent more time reading.

But despite her smoky eyes and full red lips, there's a sadness about her, especially as she lifts a Tupperware container, offering a small, practiced smile.

"I made cinnamon rolls for the guys this morning."

She doesn't have to say it. I know in an instant.

The test was negative.

She spent the morning baking because she didn't know what else to do with the disappointment.

I move without thinking, closing the space between us. Taking the container from her and setting it on the ledge of the truck, I pull her against me, enclosing her in my arms. She stiffens at first, then exhales, melting into me.

"I'm so sorry," I murmur into her hair, savoring in her familiar scent. The feel of her body against mine.

As much as I hated the idea of never losing myself in her again, I hate this more. Hate to see her hurting, feeling the quiet sadness in the way she grips onto me as if I'm the only one who can ease the pain. I'd take it all away if I could.

"I knew the chances of it working on the first try were low." Her voice is barely above a whisper. "I shouldn't have gotten my hopes up." Pulling away, she swipes at the few tears that managed to escape.

"It's okay. We'll try again…if you're still willing."

She nods. "Thank you."

"Of course."

She looks up at me, her gray eyes damp with the lingering weight of disappointment and, for a moment, I forget everything else. Why we're here. What we agreed to. How we swore this wouldn't change things.

As I hold her gaze, my attention dips to her lips — full, soft, inviting. I shouldn't be thinking about them. About how they felt beneath mine. How they parted on a quiet gasp the first time I kissed her, hesitant but needy. How she sighed into my mouth as if she'd been waiting for it just as long as I had. I shouldn't remember the way she tasted, sweet and warm, or the way her hands fisted in my shirt, pulling me closer.

But I do.

And I've missed it. Missed feeling her mouth

against mine. Missed the way she shivered when I traced my tongue along her bottom lip. Missed the quiet, desperate sounds she made when I deepened the kiss, when she pressed herself against me like she couldn't get close enough.

It's only been a matter of days, but it doesn't feel that way. Not when I still wake up remembering the way she felt wrapped around me. Not when I still catch myself staring at her, wondering if she thinks about it, too.

Would she let me kiss her now? Just for a second? Just to feel it again?

My hands twitch with the urge to frame her face, tilt her chin up, and steal the moment before she can overthink it. Before she can remind me this is just supposed to be a means to an end.

As if sensing exactly where my thoughts are going, Genevieve increases the space between us, slipping back into the businesslike composure I hate, shoulders square, head held high.

"I'll let you know when we should start trying again once I figure it out."

It shouldn't bother me. This was the agreement. But her words feel cold. Like she's scheduling an appointment with her dentist.

"Sounds good." I force a smile, pretending to be completely unaffected.

"Great."

She turns to go, but before she can take more than a few steps, I call out, "Genevieve."

She pauses, facing me again, a brow arched in anticipation. I stare at her for several long moments, unsure what to say. Why I even called out to her.

Then I erase the distance between us and wrap my arms around her again. Just like minutes ago, she briefly stiffens before melting into me, her body fitting so damn perfectly against mine.

Like we were made for each other.

But I don't say it. I don't say anything. Instead, I just hold her, relishing in the rise and fall of her chest against mine, her heart beating a steady rhythm.

Eventually, she pulls away, and I let her go, our gazes locking in silent understanding before she turns and disappears through the bay doors.

I exhale slowly, taking a moment to shake off the weight in my chest. When I turn, I find Murphy watching me with a curious expression.

"What was that all about?" he asks.

"Nothing." I grab the container of cinnamon rolls and head toward the stairs.

"Didn't look like nothing," he calls after me.

I pause and face him, leveling him with a glare. "Genevieve's dealing with something personal and wanted to talk. That's all."

It's not a complete lie. She *is* dealing with something personal. But so am I.

"If that's what you need to keep telling yourself."
He gives me a knowing smirk.

"What's that supposed to mean?"

He gestures toward where Genevieve just stood. "That wasn't just a friend consoling another friend. When are you going to stop pretending you don't have feelings for her?"

I don't answer. Because I don't know *how* to answer.

Instead, I push past him and make my way up the stairs, heading straight into the workout room, needing to do something to take my mind off everything.

TWENTY

Genevieve

I kick off my heels the moment I step inside my house, sighing as relief washes over me. My whole body aches with exhaustion. Not just from the long day, but from the weight of disappointment pressing down on me, making each step feel heavier than the last.

I knew the chances of getting pregnant the first time were low. I reminded myself of that fact over and over again. That didn't make it any easier when I stared down at that first negative test. Or the second one. Or the third.

As if that hadn't been bad enough, my period arrived this afternoon, officially cementing my disappointment.

Although there's a ray of hope mixed in with that

disappointment. Because not being pregnant means sleeping with Finn again.

I shouldn't be looking forward to it as much as I am. Shouldn't crave the way he touches me, the way he makes me feel things I have no business feeling.

But I do.

And that terrifies me more than any negative test ever could. Because what happens after another month of this? Or more?

Will I still be able to pretend this is just a means to an end? Or are we already past that? Has it already become something we both refuse to acknowledge? Should I tell him I've changed my mind before things get even more out of control?

I scrub a hand over my face and exhale deeply, trying to push the thoughts away as I strip out of my work clothes and pull on a pair of soft pajamas and an old t-shirt. Something comfortable. Something safe.

I drag myself back into the kitchen and open the refrigerator, scanning the shelves for something that might pass as dinner. I'm too tired to cook and not hungry enough to really care. The thought of ordering takeout briefly crosses my mind, but before I can act on it, a knock sounds at the front door, followed by the creak of it opening.

"Genevieve?"

I blink in surprise, stepping into the living room just as Finn slips inside.

"What are you doing here? Aren't you supposed to be on shift?"

"Destin owes me a bunch of favors. I called one in so he could cover the rest of my twenty-four." He shuts the door and steps closer, his voice softening. "Figured you might want some company."

"Finn…" I begin on a long sigh.

I don't want him to think he needs to do this sort of thing for me because we've slept together. Don't want to become dependent on him to pick up the pieces whenever I have a bad day.

Then again, Finn's always been this way — thoughtful, selfless. Always showing up when I least expect it but somehow need it most. Tonight's no different.

At least, that's what I tell myself.

"I brought reinforcements," he interjects before I can say anything, lifting the bags in his hands.

"Reinforcements?" I arch a brow.

"All the essentials. Wine, ice cream, and Mexican food." He winks as he sets them down on the coffee table.

"That's…exactly what I need tonight," I admit, physically feeling the weight lift off my shoulders.

"I know." He gives me an understanding smile, one that's steady and grounding, reminding me of the depth of our friendship.

Without a second thought, I erase the space between us and wrap my arms around him. His embrace is reassuring, and I let myself sink into him. Let myself be held for a moment. A voice in my head warns this is dangerous, that I'm toeing a line I swore I wouldn't cross. But it's just a hug. Friends hug all the time.

Except Finn's hugs have never felt like this before.

We settle onto the couch and dig into the feast he brought over — chips and salsa, *queso*, guacamole, burritos, tacos — all my favorite dishes from the local Mexican restaurant.

As we eat, Finn doesn't ask how I'm feeling after today's disappointing news. He doesn't offer hollow reassurances.

Instead, we relax on the couch and watch one of my comfort movies — *When Harry Met Sally*. He doesn't complain about it being some cheesy romcom. Doesn't ask to watch something more in line with the kind of movie he prefers. He simply sits beside me and gives me the best gift I didn't know I needed today. His presence.

When I first saw this movie, I was in complete agreement with Meg Ryan's character that men and women *can* be friends without eventually falling for each other. After all, for as long as I can remember, Finn has been my best friend. Like the characters in *When Harry Met Sally*, he's been by my side throughout all my failed relationships. Hell, he was the one I called in tears when Ethan told me he'd fallen in love with someone else and wanted a divorce.

Lately, I'm starting to wonder if maybe Billy Crystal's character was right all along. That eventually all the sex stuff gets in the way, especially if you cross that line.

Did Finn and I *really* cross that line?

It's not like we slept together on a whim and later grew to regret it, like in the movie. Our decision was intentional and came with rules and restrictions. Granted, we definitely bent some of those rules, but we haven't crossed that line since I stopped ovulating, keeping our friendship intact.

I refocus my attention on the movie, trying to think about anything other than my confusing feelings for Finn. It's nearly impossible with him mere inches away. The fact we're watching a friends-to-lovers story only serves to remind me of our relationship. Even more so now that we've slept together.

During the penultimate scene when Harry shows up at the New Year's Eve party and declares his love for Sally, I can't help but steal a glance at Finn. But he's not looking at the television. Instead, as Harry tells Sally how he loves each of her little quirks, his gaze traces over me. From my eyes. To my nose. Then to my mouth.

He licks his lips and his blue eyes darken. Much like they did earlier today at the fire station.

The room suddenly feels too warm, the air between us too charged. It would be so easy to close the distance. To press my mouth against his. To erase the lines I've been careful to draw. And for one reckless second, I almost do.

But if I kiss him, if I let myself fall into this, I won't merely blur the lines. I'll obliterate them.

And what happens when it all falls apart?

Because it will. It always does.

My marriage to Ethan is proof of that.

Reality crashes back in, and I tear my gaze away, jumping to my feet. "I should get some sleep," I say quickly. "It's been a long day."

Finn blinks, his expression unreadable. He parts his lips, and I sense he's about to tell me something important. That maybe he's about to take a page from Billy Crystal's book and declare his love after all our years of friendship.

A foolish part of me wants him to.

But he doesn't.

Instead, he pushes out a sigh and pulls himself to stand.

Approaching me, he touches a soft kiss to my cheek before making his way out of my house, leaving me alone with my conflicted thoughts about whether men and women could ever truly just be friends.

Or if this thing between Finn and me has been inevitable from the day we met.

TWENTY-ONE

Genevieve

The spa is warm and fragrant, the air filled with hints of lavender and eucalyptus as I sink into the plush chair and let my feet soak in the warm water. Beside me, Mom chats with her nail technician about the benefits of meditation and positive thinking, while Claire sits on the other side of her, flipping through a magazine on the latest celebrity gossip.

Some time with my mom and sister is exactly what I need after the disappointment of not getting pregnant. Plus, getting a massage and pedicure doesn't hurt, either. I can't remember the last time I've felt this relaxed.

"I have something for you," Mom announces as my nail technician lifts my foot out of the refreshing bath. She reaches into her oversized purse and pulls out an envelope, handing it to me with a satisfied smile.

"What's this?"

"Just open it," she encourages, her voice carrying that unmistakable note of excitement that makes me nervous. I glance past her, meeting Claire's gaze, who simply shrugs before returning her attention to her magazine.

Sighing, I open the envelope and pull out a printed image of a baby, its skin overly smooth with computer-generated perfection.

"What am I looking at?" I ask, brows knitted in confusion.

"Your baby."

"My...*baby*?"

"I did one of those online generators. Since I didn't have a picture of your sperm donor, I had to improvise a bit."

While I hate I'm not being completely honest with my mother about how I'm getting pregnant, she's never been good at keeping a secret. The last thing I need is for her to accidentally slip up about the fact that Finn will be my baby's father, considering she gets together with his mother for lunch once a week.

"I used a photo of Finn instead," she announces proudly.

I choke on my saliva, and my nail technician hands me a bottle of water. I give her a grateful smile as I take a sip, desperate to get my coughing fit under control so my mother doesn't read too much into my reaction.

"Is that right?" Claire asks Mom with a playful gleam in her eyes, no longer interested in her magazine.

"I needed something to use. Since Gen's description of the sperm donor she chose matched Finn perfectly, I used him."

"Funny about that," Claire muses, and I shoot daggers her way.

Thankfully, it goes right over our mother's head.

"I do find it interesting that Genevieve would choose a sperm donor who looks like Finn," Mom says thoughtfully.

"I don't know what he looks like," I argue. "You don't get to see a photo. It's completely anonymous. All you get is a list of their physical qualities, among other things."

It's not a complete lie. That *is* the information you get when looking for a sperm donor. I'd looked through dozens, if not hundreds, of candidates when I first started down this path. Before Finn's proposition.

"Your baby *does* look like Finn," Claire remarks, leaning over to see the photo. "You could have saved yourself the hassle and had a baby with him instead. Maybe it's not too late and you can ask him."

My skin prickles with heat, and I glare at her.

"I always thought you two would end up together," Mom sighs wistfully, oblivious to the true weight of Claire's words.

"We're just friends," I reply quickly, my voice tight.

And that's exactly what we've been this past week. Friends. Nothing more. Despite my near lapse of judgment while watching *When Harry Met Sally*.

Since then, we've fallen back into our usual rhythm — Finn bringing me coffee at the library, me stopping by the station when I know John's cooking to save them from a disaster. Everything is as it was.

Except it isn't.

Because beneath the routines we've built over the years, something feels off. An inescapable awareness now hovers in the quiet moments between us.

In the way his eyes linger on mine a second too long.

In the way his voice changes when he says my name.

It makes me wonder what it would be like if we were more than friends.

If, instead of this complicated, temporary arrangement, we were really doing this together.

Would he rub my back at night when the weight of my growing belly made sleep impossible?

Would he tease me about my cravings but still go out in the middle of the night to get whatever ridiculous thing I wanted?

Would he look at me with that same sincerity in

his eyes he had when he told me he wanted this? When he promised he was all in?

A hint of something warm, something dangerously hopeful, stirs deep in my chest, but I quickly push it down.

I can't let myself think like this.

Because I've been here before.

And I can't go back there. Not for anyone.

Including Finn.

With our bodies relaxed and nails painted various shades, we leave the spa and make our way down a charming shopping area in Tahoe. It's a beautiful summer day, so the streets are filled with tourists here to enjoy the outdoor activities this area is known for.

As we meander down the sidewalk, trying to decide on a place for a late lunch, Mom halts in front of a boutique, her eyes lighting up.

"We have to go in!"

I hesitate as I take in the front windows filled with baby clothes. "I don't think I should."

"It'll be good for you," she insists, wrapping her hand around my wrist. "You need to release positive energy into the universe and open yourself up to getting pregnant. If you act like you already are, the universe will give you what you want."

Claire raises a skeptical brow. "Can I tell the

universe I want a million dollars and a hot guy? Order it up like DoorDash?"

Mom gives her a patient smile. "If you don't believe in it, it won't happen. But if you open yourself up to the idea and are willing to accept the gifts the universe is ready to bestow on you, then yes. You can ask the universe to deliver these things."

Claire smirks. "Sweet. Universe…" She looks toward the sky. "I'd like a million dollars and a really hot guy capable of multiple Os."

Mom sighs but doesn't rise to the bait. "Poke fun all you want, Claire, but it works. I put becoming a grandmother on my vision board for the year, and a few months later, Genevieve told me she wanted to have a baby. The universe knows."

I roll my eyes but allow my mother to drag me inside, though unease creeps along my spine.

The store smells like fresh cotton and lavender, and the soft chime of the boutique door makes me feel like I'm intruding on a world I don't quite belong to yet. The space is small but beautiful, filled with delicate, cream-colored bassinets, plush blankets, and racks of impossibly tiny clothes. A mother-to-be browses near the back, her hands cradling her belly as her partner murmurs something that makes her laugh.

I don't belong here.

I *shouldn't* be here.

But then Mom squeezes my hand, letting me

know with a single look I have every right to be here. She encourages me farther into the shop and, after a few minutes, I start to breathe a little easier. The onesies aren't as daunting anymore. The idea of holding a baby I call my own doesn't feel like some faraway dream.

I've avoided looking at baby clothes or furniture because I was worried it would be too painful. Now as I imagine dressing my baby in a cute dress or a dapper suit, it makes me believe this might actually happen for me. I even let Mom buy a gender-neutral onesie, though she wanted to buy a whole wardrobe.

Maybe this onesie will be *my* vision board. This year, a baby is all I want.

When my mom hands me the bag with my first article of baby clothing, I feel lighter than I have in a while. Like I'm finally on the right path.

With my head held high, I start toward the door, standing to the side as another couple enters. I smile at the woman, her belly round with pregnancy. A warmth fills me as I imagine myself in her place in a few months.

But when I see the man beside her, my smile instantly falls.

The world around me dulls, the present blurring into the past as a memory slams into me.

Ethan and me standing in a store much like this one in San Francisco, his hand resting on my lower back as I reached for a tiny onesie that read "Little

Bookworm". I remember the way he laughed, low and warm, pressing a kiss to my temple as he murmured, "One day, baby. One day."

I believed him. I believed all his promises.

Now he's here with *her*. My replacement. A ring on her finger. Carrying the child *we* once talked about having.

"Genevieve," Ethan exhales, just as surprised to see me.

A lump rises in my throat from hearing his voice again after all this time, but I swallow it down, forcing myself to meet his gaze.

"Ethan."

"It's been a while." He clears his throat.

"It has."

Silence stretches between us, thick and suffocating.

Ethan recovers first, turning toward the woman at his side. "This is Rebecca. Rebecca, this is Genevieve." He hesitates. "And her mom, Judy, and sister, Claire." He gestures to the two women flanking me like a disapproving army.

Claire shifts beside me, crossing her arms over her chest in a way that screams hostile witness. Mom, to her credit, plasters on a pleasant, if somewhat strained, smile.

"It's nice to meet you," Rebecca says sweetly.

She's effortlessly beautiful. Warm brown eyes,

shiny caramel-blonde hair, the kind of glow that comes from being adored…and pregnant.

Her belly rounds beneath a fitted dress that emphasizes rather than hides, like she's embracing every part of this journey. One hand rests on her stomach, the other looped casually through Ethan's arm.

A sharp pang cuts through me before I can stop it.

I should have been the one on Ethan's arm carrying his baby. We should have been laughing and smiling at each other as we picked out baby clothes together. I should have been fighting with him over what color to paint the nursery.

Instead, I'll do all of that alone.

"Ethan told me a lot about you." Rebecca offers me a perfect, practiced smile.

I wonder which version of me he told her about. The one he loved? Or the one he left?

"I wish I could say the same," I murmur before I can filter the words.

Claire bites back a laugh, and Mom presses her lips together like she's trying to keep from saying something much less polite.

"So, uh…" Ethan clears his throat again, shifting on his feet, "what brings you here?"

"Genevieve's trying to get pregnant," Mom chimes in.

If there were a trapdoor beneath me, I'd pull the lever myself.

Ethan's eyebrows shoot up, his gaze instinctively flicking to my ringless hand. "I didn't realize you'd remarried."

I lift my chin. "I don't need a husband to have a baby. I'm more than capable of doing it on my own. In fact, all things considered, I prefer it. That way, I don't have to worry about the man who swore he'd always love me coming home and telling me it was all a lie."

Ethan winces in response to my words, and another awkward silence falls between us. Rebecca doesn't let it linger for long, trying to break the tension as if she's not the cause of it.

"That's so brave." She rests a hand on her belly. "I don't know what I'd do without Ethan helping me through the pregnancy. Especially the first trimester. I was so sick."

The words hit like a gut punch.

Not just because she's pregnant with Ethan's child, but because it's him — his voice, his touch, his presence — who's helping her through it.

That should have been me he was helping through those difficult first few weeks.

Mom must sense the shift in me because she claps a hand on my shoulder and offers Rebecca a polite, but pointed, smile. "It appears us Thomas women are made of much tougher stuff. Have a nice day."

She steers Claire and me away before I can say anything else, not stopping until we're a block away.

Then she reaches into her purse and starts aggressively spraying something around me.

I cough at the overwhelming scent. "What is that?" I grab the bottle and squint at the label. "Evil Be Gone?"

Claire chokes on a laugh, and Mom huffs. "You don't need that man's energy in your life. Not if you're trying to have a baby." She grips my shoulders, firm and steady, forcing me to meet her gaze. "And you *will* have a baby, Gen. I know it. And you'll give him or her all the love they need. You'll be enough. You *are* enough. Do you understand?"

I swallow hard as I melt into my mother's embrace, grateful she always knows what I need to hear. I can only hope I'm half the mother she's always been.

"Thanks, Mom."

"Of course, sweetie." She pulls back, meeting my gaze. "Now, what do you say to a bit of day drinking?"

I blow out a laugh. "That sounds amazing."

TWENTY-TWO

Finn

"Genevieve?" My voice echoes through her quiet house as I let myself in, knocking lightly to announce my presence.

She doesn't answer. No playful retort, no hurried promise that she just needs five more minutes to finish getting ready. Nothing.

I find her on the couch, legs crossed, dressed in pajamas —= cotton shorts and an oversized T-shirt that's slipping off one shoulder.

But it's not her clothes that stop me in my tracks. It's the tiny onesie on the coffee table in front of her.

My heart lurches, thoughts spinning in a dozen different directions.

Is she pregnant after all? Were the tests she took wrong?

I never actually asked if she got her period. I just assumed she had, since she told me when we'd need to start trying again. She wouldn't know that unless she'd gotten her period, right?

But if she's not pregnant, why is she staring at that tiny piece of fabric like it holds all the answers?

And if she *is* pregnant, why does she look like someone just told her that her cat was hit by a car?

"Genevieve?" My voice is cautious, careful.

She blinks, finally seeming to notice I'm here.

"Is there something you need to tell me?" I ask, unsure what I want her to say.

Actually, I *know* what I want her to say.

As much as I want to give her the baby she's always dreamed of, I don't want this to be over yet. Whatever *this* is.

"My mom thought it might help," she explains with a subtle roll of her eyes. "She claims if I bought some baby clothes, I'd be letting the universe know I'm ready to receive its gift of a baby."

I chuckle, pushing down any sign of relief over the fact that she's not pregnant. I should have known her mother would have something to do with it.

"Why am I not surprised?" I lower myself onto the couch beside her. But she still doesn't look at me. She's not really looking at the onesie, either. She's looking past it.

Past everything.

"What's wrong, Genevieve?" I ask softly, praying

she's not about to tell me having this onesie in her house has caused her to have a change of heart.

After several protracted moments, she finally brings her eyes to mine and parts her lips, her response on the tip of her tongue. But then she shakes her head.

"Nothing. It's nothing," she says, although I get the feeling it's more for her benefit than mine. Then she furrows her brow. "What are you doing here? Not that I mind you stopping by. I just wasn't expecting you."

I give her a pointed stare. "Jude's bowling tournament? You said you wanted to go."

"Shit." She squeezes her eyes shut. "I completely forgot." She springs up from the couch and hurries toward her bedroom. "Give me five minutes to get dressed."

As I watch her go, I can't shake the feeling something is off with her. I pull myself to my feet and follow her down the hallway.

"Are you sure you're okay?" I lean against the doorframe, watching as she rummages through her closet.

"Of course," she insists, not facing me. "Why wouldn't I be okay? It's not like I ran into my ex-husband today while he was with his brand-new wife." She slides hanger after hanger down the railing, each one being moved with increasing force. "His brand-new, *pregnant* wife."

"Shit, Gen." I push off the doorframe, making my way toward her.

"It doesn't matter," she continues, yanking a hanger free. "He doesn't matter. He——"

Her voice catches.

I don't think she realizes how hard she's gripping the hanger in her hands until I gently pry it away and pull her into my arms.

For a second, she stays stiff, fighting it.

Then she caves.

Her body sags against mine, and a broken sound escapes her lips. Not quite a sob, but damn close.

I tighten my hold on her, hating I wasn't there when she saw him. Hating she's been sitting in this house, stewing in this alone.

"Listen to me, Genevieve." I tilt her chin, forcing her to meet my gaze. "Don't give this to him. Ethan was a fucking idiot. I thought it when I first met him, and I think it even more today. He wasn't nearly good enough for you. He didn't deserve you. And he sure as shit doesn't deserve your tears."

A weak, watery laugh escapes her throat, and I swipe my thumbs over her damp cheeks.

"What you're doing is incredible."

"Is it?" she asks weakly. "Or am I just being self-ish? Wanting to have a baby, knowing it won't be easy doing it on my own?"

"What makes you think you'll be alone?"

She lets out a humorless laugh. "I *am* alone."

I shake my head, my grip on her tightening. "You have your mom. Your sister. And me."

She swallows, her lips parting like she wants to argue, remind me of the role I'll play in her baby's life. And the role I won't be allowed to play.

But I don't let her.

"What you're doing isn't selfish, Genevieve. It's one of the most selfless acts I can think of. You have so much love to give, and you're willing to do whatever it takes to share that love with a tiny human." My fingers tighten on her face. "That's why I wanted you to choose me. Because I wanted to be a part of something good. Something I can be proud of. Something worthwhile."

She stares at me for several long moments, my words echoing around us. My eyes drop to her lips and the air between us changes, becoming charged.

I want to kiss her. God, do I want to kiss her. But I agreed to the rules, so I reluctantly release her from my grasp and increase the distance between us before I do something I can't take back.

Something that destroys our friendship.

"You should—"

Genevieve cuts me off with a harsh grip to my cheeks. Then she slams her mouth to mine.

For a second, I freeze, completely caught off guard.

It's not the first time we've kissed. Hell, by this point, I could probably draw her lips from memory.

But this kiss feels…different. More raw. More real. It's not a means to an end, the end being her bed so she can hopefully get pregnant.

Instead, she's kissing me because she *wants* to.

At least, I *hope* she wants to.

Before I have a chance to return her kiss, she tears her mouth from mine and jumps back, keeping her eyes averted.

"I… I'm not sure what came over me." She turns toward the closet again to hide her flushed cheeks. "Just give me a minute to get dressed."

I should leave.

Give her space.

Pretend she didn't just kiss me outside of our arrangement. That's what a good man would do. What a *decent* man would do.

But all I can think about is how fucking perfect Genevieve's lips felt on mine just now.

And I want more.

Eating up the space between us, I wrap my fingers around her arm, forcing her toward me. On a sharp inhale, she flings her wide eyes to mine, a question within.

Or maybe a challenge.

Licking my lips, I slowly bring my mouth closer to hers, every inch I erase feeling like miles. But I want to give her a chance to stop this runaway train before I happily drive it off its tracks.

Which is exactly what she does as my lips are

about to meet hers, a hand to my chest forcing me to pause.

"What about our agreement?" she asks softly. "The rules?"

"I've never wanted to break the rules more than I do right now, Genevieve," I answer honestly.

She searches my eyes for several long moments, neither retreating nor advancing. I expect for her to remind me I agreed to her limitations. That if we do this, it will blur whatever lines remain between us. After all, Genevieve's a rule follower by nature. I doubt she'd break the rules now, especially with our friendship on the line.

Then a wicked smile curves across her lips and she lifts onto her toes, only a breath between us.

"Let's break some rules, Finn," she says before crashing her mouth back to mine.

TWENTY-THREE

Genevieve

This is a bad idea.

I know it is.

There are dozens — no, hundreds — of reasons I should stop this. Right now.

But none of them compare to the one reason I can't.

Because the thought of depriving myself of this, of *him*, feels unbearable.

After today, after seeing Ethan and his picture-perfect wife carrying his child, I need to feel something else. *Anything* else. I need something to drown out the ache clawing at my chest, asking if I've ever been enough for anyone.

Now, with Finn's lips pressed against mine, his body flush with mine, Ethan and his pregnant wife are the last things on my mind. Right now, all I can think about is experiencing the incredible sensations only this man has been able to bring out of me.

"Finn," I whimper as he peels his lips away from mine and peppers kisses along the column of my neck.

"Yes?" He slips his hands under my shirt, causing a shiver to trickle down my spine.

"What about your brother's bowling tournament?"

He hesitates, but doesn't immediately pull back. Eventually, he brings his eyes to mine.

"Do you honestly think that, given the choice between you and Jude's tournament, I'd want to spend my night in an antiquated bowling alley surrounded by the smell of fried food and stale beer?"

I shrug. "I didn't want to assume anything. And I don't want to interfere with your plans. I—"

"Stop," he interjects before I can utter another word. "If I didn't want to be with you, I wouldn't be here." He brings his lips closer. "But I have a confession to make…"

"What's that?" My voice comes out low and rough.

"I'll always choose you, Genevieve." His lips brush mine, so soft and reverent it makes my throat tighten. "Always."

The word burrows deep inside me, unearthing emotions I'm not ready to name. Because I know what happens when someone makes you believe in forever. I know how it feels when forever turns into a lie.

But Finn isn't Ethan.

And right now, I don't want to think. I don't want to analyze what this means. Whether I'll regret it later. Whether this will inevitably change us.

I just want to feel.

"Always," I whisper, the word slipping past my lips before Finn crashes into me.

His kiss is hot and desperate, his tongue sweeping against mine in a seductive dance I'm powerless to resist. And I don't want to, either.

"Red or green light?" Finn murmurs as he slides his hand up my shirt, pausing just shy of my bra.

I hesitate. Not because I don't want this, but because I want it *too* much. Want *him* too much.

"Red or green light?" he repeats, ghosting his thumb over my covered nipple.

At the subtle touch, I try to swallow down the whimper begging to escape, but it's a losing battle.

It always is with him.

"Green light," I exhale.

"Thank fuck."

He slams his lips back against mine in a heated kiss before pulling back and ripping my t-shirt over my head. He wastes no time in ridding himself of his shirt, then reaches behind me, unclasping my bra and tossing it to the floor.

I should feel exposed. Vulnerable.

But I don't.

Not with the way he looks at me. Like I'm the only thing he's ever wanted. Like he'd burn down the world for me if I asked him to.

He leans toward me, his lips brushing mine as his finger skims over my nipple.

"Finn," I moan, consumed with the sensations flowing through me.

"What do you need?"

"More." I pull him closer, dragging my fingers through his hair. "More of your mouth. Your teeth. Everything."

"You got it."

His lips move against mine as he grips my hip and steers me the few feet toward the bed before gently lowering me onto the surface. He snakes down my body, taking his time to worship every inch of me. When he reaches my breast, he pauses again, shifting his gaze to mine.

"Red light or green light?" he asks once more.

"Green," I say without hesitation.

"Good girl."

With a smirk, he covers my nipple with his mouth, and I release a sigh, which turns into a yelp when he gently bites on the sensitive bud. It's painful yet exhilarating at the same time, increasing the ache that overwhelms me whenever I'm with Finn.

He trails his tongue between my breasts, his

fingers teasing both nipples as he slowly travels down my torso, stopping when he reaches the waistband of my shorts. He drags his tongue along the skin by the material, his eyes drifting to meet mine again.

"Red or green light?"

"Green." My hasty response earns me another sexy smirk.

He hooks his fingers into the waistband, and I eagerly lift my hips, allowing him to slide my shorts down my legs along with my panties.

When he returns to me, he pushes my thighs wide, his eyes dripping with lust as he takes me in.

"Red or green?" he asks again, his chest heaving as if he's struggling to maintain his control.

I am, too.

"Green."

The word's barely fallen from my lips when his mouth is on me. I instantly melt into the mattress, the feel of him swirling his tongue against my clit turning my body to mush.

"God, I've missed this," I exhale as I run my fingers through his hair, my confession leaving before I can stop it.

"I've missed this, too," he hums against me. "Missed how amazing you taste. Missed the way you move." He slides a finger inside me. "Missed how greedy this cunt is for me."

"Finn," I moan, fire heating my veins in response to the combination of his ministrations and words.

"Have you gotten yourself off since the last time we were together?" he asks, adding another finger and stretching me out even more.

"I…" I trail off, words escaping me.

He stops his motions, and I fling my wide eyes toward him, his lack of touch akin to torture.

"Tell me," he says with a sly smirk, knowing all too well how tightly wound I am. "Give me what I need and I'll give you what *you* need."

"Yes."

"Yes?" He arches a brow.

"Yes, I've gotten myself off since the last time we were together."

"While I hate I'm not the last person to make you come, the image of you getting yourself off is a fucking turn on."

He returns his mouth to me, inserting his fingers inside me once more.

"Tell me this, Genevieve. What did you think about?"

It's one thing to confess I've touched myself, and quite frequently, in the short time since we were last intimate. It's another to admit that, every time, I replayed all the things he did to me. But even if I don't admit it, he'll know. He always does.

"You," I confess. "I thought about you."

"I've thought about you every time I've jerked off, too," he murmurs, his rhythm growing more desperate as he completely consumes me with his mouth.

"Oh, god…"

I shouldn't find any satisfaction over the idea that he's jerked off while thinking of me. This is my best friend. Friends don't think about each other like this. And they certainly don't get themselves off to the memory of being with each other.

But that's precisely what I've done.

And it sounds like Finn's just as guilty.

"That's it, baby. Let go. Let me feel you."

The combination of his motions and his voice is my undoing. Any restraint I was able to hold on to is obliterated when Finn nibbles on my clit, the warring sensations pushing me over the edge.

But unlike so many other times, Finn doesn't milk my orgasm.

He's on his feet in a heartbeat, shoving his shorts and boxer briefs down his legs before returning to the bed and bringing his erection up to me.

"Red or green," he pants through a tight jaw as he teases me with his arousal.

"Green. It's all fucking green."

My response has barely left my mouth when he thrusts into me, both of us crying out in ecstasy.

"Fucking perfect," Finn declares, not moving, savoring in the sensation of fullness after too long without it.

Wrapping my legs around his waist, I cling to him,

never wanting to let go. Never wanting to leave this place. This moment. This feeling of completeness.

"I've missed this, too," I murmur, taking his earlobe between my teeth. "So damn much."

"So damn much," he repeats as he starts to move.

His lips cover mine, his tongue exploring my mouth as he sensually rocks his hips against me, drawing out every tiny little sensation. Every tremor. Every ripple. Every gasp.

Nothing's ever felt so damn right, yet so damn confusing at the same time.

But I refuse to worry about that. I can't. Not when I've never felt anything as incredible as Finn's body moving in time with me, pushing me higher and higher until I can no longer fight it and fall over the edge with him.

TWENTY-FOUR

Finn

I wake up to the comforting scent of cinnamon and sugar, relishing in the warmth of the bed. But that fades fast when I reach for Genevieve and find nothing but cool sheets.

I don't know what I expected. Waking up to her curled against me, her body still tangled with mine?

Maybe.

Now that it's morning, the weight of last night presses against me. I can't decide if it was a colossal mistake or an inevitability.

If *Genevieve* will think it was a colossal mistake or an inevitability.

I scrub a hand down my face before pulling on my boxer briefs, following the sound of soft clinks and the occasional rustle of parchment paper coming from the kitchen. Sure enough, Genevieve's baking. She always bakes when she wants to keep her hands busy. To distract herself from something she doesn't want to think about.

Like what we did last night.

I lean against the counter and watch as she scoops the batter into muffin tins, her movements controlled.

Too controlled.

"'Morning," I say, testing the waters.

She doesn't look up. "'Morning."

"How are you?" I ask, resisting the urge to wrap her in my arms and press tender kisses to the soft skin of her neck. It's obvious she's still working through last night in her head so I keep my distance.

For now.

"Fine."

I don't believe her for a second.

I should let it go. Let her pretend. But *I* can't pretend.

Not after last night.

I step closer, careful not to touch her yet, but close enough to see the tension in her shoulders. "Do you want to talk about it?"

She finally pauses, gripping the scoop a little too tightly before answering. "What's there to talk about?"

"We broke some boundaries last night."

"I know." She finally meets my gaze. "I was there."

This is classic Genevieve. Deflecting. Brushing it

off. Tucking her emotions neatly into compartments and locking them away so she can pretend it didn't mean anything.

Pretend she didn't feel anything.

But *I* felt it. Every incredible second.

Hell, I still feel it.

"Genevieve…" I narrow my gaze on her, refusing to let her avoid this conversation.

And she knows it.

Finally, she pushes out a long sigh. "It's not the first time we've slept together, Finn. You *are* trying to get me pregnant."

Her voice is casual, but there's something in her eyes. A hint of something she doesn't want me to see.

Last night wasn't just another night for her, either.

It meant something, even if she'll never admit it to herself or anyone else.

"I'm just trying to figure out where your head's at. That's all."

She hesitates as she's about to scoop more batter into the tin. Then she admits, "I don't know." She slowly lifts her gaze toward mine. "Where's *your* head?"

I open my mouth, but don't immediately respond.

Because the truth is, I don't fucking know, either.

Last night wasn't just sex. It wasn't about the damn schedule or the agreement we made.

It was about *her*.

Her nails scraping down my back.

Her voice breaking on my name.

The way she looked at me like I was the only thing keeping her from unraveling completely.

Now, in the light of day, I don't know what that means.

But I know one thing. I want more of it. More of her.

I take a hesitant step toward her, studying her reaction for any sign of reluctance. Thankfully, she doesn't retreat, allowing me to invade her space.

"I really enjoyed last night. It was nice not to be under any…pressure."

Something in her posture relaxes, her lips parting slightly. "Me, too."

"So maybe we take the pressure off each other."

She tilts her head. "How so?"

"Maybe we stop being so…clinical about it. I read a few threads on Reddit about this." I scratch the back of my neck. "A lot of women mentioned they didn't get pregnant until they stopped being so focused on the calendar. Some think it was the stress of it all that affected them, and once they stopped…forcing it, it worked.

Her brows shoot up. "You went on Reddit looking for pregnancy tips?"

"I was just trying to educate myself," I argue in my defense. "Maybe that's what we do, too. Maybe we stop forcing it. Stop living by a calendar."

She leans a hip against the counter, crossing her

arms. "So you're suggesting we…what? Have sex whenever we want?"

"Sure." I clear my throat, feeling more nervous now than I was the first time I asked out a girl. "I just…" I run a hand through my hair to collect my thoughts. "This shouldn't be stressful for you, Genevieve. Maybe we just sleep together whenever the mood strikes and not be so focused on making sure I'm fucking you at the exact right time on the exact right day."

"So we'll sleep together any time?" she asks yet again, as if not fully grasping the concept.

"Yes."

"As friends?" She studies me, searching my face for something.

"Of course." I swallow, my throat suddenly dry. "Nothing else in our original agreement will change."

I don't know if I'm saying this to get her to agree or to rationalize my own feelings. Probably both.

"We just won't be so rigid about *when* we have sex."

She looks past me, deep in thought.

This is when she'll tell me it's a horrible idea.

Because it *is* a horrible idea.

But being with Genevieve is unlike anything I've experienced in my life. Despite all the reasons I should do everything to keep the lines between us drawn, I want this.

I want *her*.

Finally, she looks back at me and gives a small nod. "Okay."

I blink, convinced I misheard her. "Okay?"

"Yes. No more scheduling sex. We sleep together whenever we're in the mood," she says very matter-of-factly before turning back around and scooping more batter into the muffin tins.

I watch her, my gaze drifting down the curve of her back. The little boy shorts clinging to her hips. The faint bite marks on her shoulder blades… Marks *I* left.

Heat flares inside me, possessive and dangerous and so fucking reckless.

I step behind her, sliding an arm around her waist and pulling her against me so she can feel exactly what she does to me.

She releases a soft whimper, melting into me.

I lower my lips to her ear, my voice husky as I say, "I'm kind of in the mood now."

She slowly turns in my arms and runs her fingers into my hair, a flirtatious smile curving her lips.

"I was hoping you'd say that."

Then her mouth crashes against mine.

TWENTY-FIVE

Genevieve

I stare blankly at the spreadsheet open on my computer screen, the budget numbers blurring together into an incoherent mess. I should be preparing for my meeting, double-checking figures, making sure I have all the necessary information.

Instead, all I can think about is Finn.

Correction.

All I can think about is *sex* with Finn.

Heat floods my skin at the mere thought, a slow burn that pools low in my belly, tightening with need. A need I should be able to ignore. A need I used to ignore.

We agreed to stop looking at the calendar to take the pressure off. Apparently, that means we can't keep our hands off each other.

Since Finn showed up at my house Saturday evening, we barely left my bed. The only reason we did was to eat and for him to go feed Duke before we ended up tangled in the sheets again.

I shift in my chair and press my thighs together at the reminder. It does nothing to dull the ache. My body is still sore from our weekend of marathon sex. Yet, I want more.

I fear I always will.

That's not supposed to be the case. I was supposed to be pragmatic about this arrangement, clear-eyed and logical. No emotions. No complications. No straying from the rules.

We didn't just stray from the rules this weekend. We completely obliterated them.

And instead of insisting we return to our original agreement, I eagerly accepted Finn's new proposal. Proof that I'm becoming far too addicted to him.

But I *am* an adult. I can separate my feelings from what happens in bed.

Right?

I glance at the clock on the wall, noting I have to leave for my meeting in fifteen minutes. If I leave now, I could swing by Finn's place for a quickie. Just enough to take the edge off.

Except I know the truth.

I'd never be satisfied with a quickie. I'd want more.

A sharp knock at my office door startles me. I

straighten, forcing my expression into something neutral, expecting one of my staff members.

But it's not.

Finn's broad frame fills the doorway, the sight of him stealing the air from my lungs. The navy blue t-shirt stretches across his chest, hinting at the solid muscle beneath, while his cargo shorts sit low on his hips, drawing my attention exactly where it shouldn't go. His jaw is rough with scruff, and I can feel the phantom scrape of it against my skin.

"Maybe manifestation really does work," I murmur, a teasing smirk curving my lips.

"What makes you say that?" The intensity in his eyes is like a magnet, pulling me in, sending a pulse of heat straight between my legs.

I push out of my chair, crossing the small space toward him. "I was just thinking about you, and now here you are."

"What were you thinking about?"

"Technically, not *you*." My voice drops to something softer, something teasing. "More like your cock."

"Do you only like me for my cock?"

I shrug. "That… And your sperm."

He loops an arm around my waist and pulls me flush against him. "I should feel used."

"But you don't."

He slowly shakes his head, his gaze floating to my lips. "No, I don't."

And then he kisses me.

It's immediate, urgent, like he's been craving me just as much as I've been craving him. My fingers thread into his hair, tugging lightly as his hands slide lower, gripping my ass, forcing me against his hard length. A desperate sound escapes me, and he takes full advantage, deepening the kiss, capturing my breath, consuming me completely.

"I've always wanted to do this," he rasps, kicking the door shut behind him.

"What's that?" I pant as he buries his head in the crook of my neck, his unshaven jawline invigorating on my flesh.

"Bend you over your desk and fuck you."

A thrill shoots through me.

This is definitely getting out of hand.

And I should stop it.

But instead, I rise onto my toes and brush my lips against his. "Then what are you waiting for?"

With a growl, he slams his mouth back to mine, our tongues tangling in a dance I feel all over my body. Too soon, he abruptly pulls out of the kiss and spins me around, bending me over the surface of my desk, papers and pens going flying.

"Good thing you're wearing this dress." He runs a hand up my leg, my muscles tightening as he nears the place I'm desperate to feel him. "I think we should add this to your list of rules."

"Add what?" I glance over my shoulder as he

lowers his zipper, the heat in his stare almost too much.

"That you're required to wear a dress to work every day."

"Any reason for that?"

"So I can fuck you anytime I want." He pushes my panties to the side and brings his erection up to me.

When he thrusts into me, I have to fight back the scream begging to be set free. I'm already on dangerous ground here. The last thing I need is to bring even more attention to what I'm doing by screaming Finn's name.

"God, you're incredible," he grunts, his grip on my hips tightening as he drives in and out of me with an urgency I've never experienced. "You take my cock so damn good. I love watching me slide in and out of you. Seeing how wet you get for me. How greedy this pussy is for me."

"Finn," I moan, overwhelmed by his motions and words.

He smooths a hand along my backside, pushing the skirt of my dress up to my waist.

"It's made me think."

"What's that?" I ask, glancing over my shoulder once more and meeting his gaze.

"If your pussy is this greedy for me," he begins, sliding his hand over my flesh, "how would you react if I touched you here?"

He brings a hand to my clit. I'm about to remind him he's already touched me there countless times when he pulls his finger back and brings it up to the puckered flesh of my ass.

"Red or green?" he asks in a low, raspy voice.

My pulse increases, a million different thoughts filling me. No one's ever touched me there. But I want this. Want to experience everything I can with him.

"Green," I pant, my breathing ragged.

"Good girl," Finn praises as he slowly eases a finger inside, drawing a moan from me.

I try to stay quiet, but it's impossible with the unique sensations filling me. It's all too much, yet not enough.

"You should see yourself, Genevieve," he grunts, his motions increasing with desperation. "My cock fucking your pussy." He leans over me and bites my earlobe. "My finger fucking your ass."

I release a whimper, on the verge of shattering into thousands of pieces.

"You like that, don't you? Like me filling both your holes."

"God, yes."

"Before this is over, I'm going to take you here, too." He pushes his finger in and out of me with more urgency. "Can I do that? Can I fuck your ass?"

I'm so blissed out from sensation that I can barely put together a coherent thought. But the truth is, I want that with Finn. Want him to push me to my limits. Past my limits. Want to give myself over to him in every way possible.

Want him to *own* me in every way possible.

Except the one way that really matters.

"Yes," comes my garbled reply.

"What's that?"

"Yes, Finn. Yes, I want you to fuck my ass."

"And I will. When you're ready. For now, I want you to come all over my cock."

He doesn't have to ask twice. Between the relentless drives of his dick and the tempting circles of his finger, I'm putty in his hands, shockwaves rushing through me as I come undone around him.

"Fuck, Gen," he grunts as he picks up the pace. "Feeling your pussy and ass clench around me. My god. I've never felt this before. Never needed anyone as bad as I need you. Tell me you're mine."

"I'm yours," I exhale, my body consumed with tremors from the orgasm still ravaging me.

"Tell me this cunt is mine."

"My cunt is yours."

He circles my ass with his finger. "What about here?"

"It's yours, too. Every inch of me is yours, Finn. You own me."

"Oh, fuck," he exhales, his motions growing even more frenzied. Then he curves over me, his teeth clamping on my neck to muffle his cries as he jerks through his release.

Neither one of us moves for several long moments, the only sound in the office that of our ragged breathing.

Finally, he gradually pulls out of me, then helps me straighten. As he does, he presses his mouth against mine, his kiss soft and gentle, at complete odds with the way he just fucked me.

"Are you okay?" He cups my cheeks, forcing my eyes to his. "It wasn't too much, was it?"

A lazy grin crawls on my lips. "I gave you the green light." I hoist myself onto my toes, chasing his kiss. But before I can touch my mouth to his, he stops me.

"I just want to make sure you don't have any regrets."

"None." I bite my lower lip. "I like when you take control. When you talk about using me. I probably shouldn't but—"

"Who says?"

A shrug is my only response.

"Listen to me, Gen." He tightens his grip on my face. "There's nothing wrong with having certain cravings or fantasies. I'm sorry you spent so much time with someone who made you feel there was. You won't get that with me. You want to give up control for a little while and explore these desires? I'm more than happy to give that to you." His mouth slowly descends toward me.

I pull him closer, giving serious consideration to

the idea of taking the rest of the day off so we can go back to my place and explore even more of my fantasies.

But before I can suggest it, the alarm on my phone goes off, cutting the moment short.

"I need to go," I say with a groan. "I have a budget meeting at town hall."

"Don't let me keep you, then." Finn steps back, giving me space to adjust my dress.

I reach for a tissue, but he wraps a hand around my wrist, stopping me.

"Don't."

I furrow my brow, confused.

"I want you to go to that meeting with my scent all over you. With my come dripping from you, reminding you of where I was." He leans closer, his breath hot on my skin. "Reminding you that I own this pussy." He dips a finger under my dress, pushing my panties aside and teasing me. Then he glides it up my backside, toying with me there. "And this ass."

I moan, gently pulsing against him, desperate to feel him everywhere.

But he quickly releases me, making me long for his touch.

I take a minute to smooth my hair and adjust my dress, doing my best to look like I wasn't just thoroughly fucked by my best friend.

My best friend.

The words should be all the reminder I need to put some distance between us.

But all they do is send a shiver down my spine because, right now, Finn doesn't feel like my best friend. He feels like something else entirely. Something dangerous. Something I can't seem to quit.

Once I'm confident I look somewhat presentable, we step out of my office and into the library, Finn at my side.

I'm probably imagining it, but I swear every set of eyes drifts to us, as if they all somehow know exactly what we were doing behind my closed office door. It's irrational. My office is tucked away at the end of the administrative hallway, where only staff are allowed. There's no way anyone could know.

And yet, I feel exposed. As if what we're doing, what we've *been* doing, is written all over me.

When we finally step outside, I inhale deeply, letting the fresh air clear my head. Space. I need space from Finn. From this. From the way my body still hums in satisfaction while my mind screams at me to get a grip.

But I don't get my wish.

Before I can open my car door, Finn cages me against it, his body a wall of heat, his presence all-consuming.

"Can I see you tonight? Maybe bring Duke over so I don't have to worry about leaving early to feed him."

A voice in the back of my mind tells me I'm losing control of the situation. But Finn is a drug, and I'm already craving my next hit.

Besides, this could be our last month together. I may as well take advantage of it.

At least that's what I tell myself so I don't have to justify why I nod instead of tell him no.

"I'd like that."

I'm rewarded with his enigmatic grin, and he begins to retreat, giving me space to get into my car. But then he grabs my arm, tugging me back against him and capturing my mouth in a kiss.

I freeze.

Not because I don't want it. But because this is different.

Finn has kissed me plenty of times. But never like this. Never out in the open, in the middle of historic downtown, where anyone can see.

It's reckless.

It's dangerous.

It's everything I swore I wasn't going to let this become.

And yet, I don't push him away.

Because for one fleeting moment, I let myself pretend that Finn kissing me outside my place of employment isn't a risk. That it isn't a complication.

Instead, I pretend I could give him everything he needs. Everything he deserves.

Even if, in my heart, I know I never can.

TWENTY-SIX

Finn

I don't know when this thing between Genevieve and me became purely sex, but that's what it feels like now.

It's not that I don't enjoy it.

I fucking love every second of it.

But I don't want her to think that's all I care about. Don't want to lose sight of what makes us…*us*.

Which is why I'm standing in her kitchen on a Friday night, tasting the sauce of the IndiI stare blankly at the spreadsheet open on my computer screen, the budget numbers blurring together into an incoherent mess. I should be preparing for my meeting, double-checking figures, making sure I have all the necessary information.

Instead, all I can think about is Finn.

Correction.

All I can think about is *sex* with Finn.

Heat floods my skin at the mere thought, a slow burn that pools low in my belly, tightening with need. A need I should be able to ignore. A need I used to ignore.

We agreed to stop looking at the calendar to take the pressure off. Apparently, that means we can't keep our hands off each other.

Since Finn showed up at my house Saturday evening, we barely left my bed. The only reason we did was to eat and for him to go feed Duke before we ended up tangled in the sheets again.

I shift in my chair and press my thighs together at the reminder. It does nothing to dull the ache. My body is still sore from our weekend of marathon sex. Yet, I want more.

I fear I always will.

That's not supposed to be the case. I was supposed to be pragmatic about this arrangement, clear-eyed and logical. No emotions. No complications. No straying from the rules.

We didn't just stray from the rules this weekend. We completely obliterated them.

And instead of insisting we return to our original agreement, I eagerly accepted Finn's new proposal. Proof that I'm becoming far too addicted to him.

But I *am* an adult. I can separate my feelings from what happens in bed.

Right?

I glance at the clock on the wall, noting I have to leave for my meeting in fifteen minutes. If I leave now, I could swing by Finn's place for a quickie. Just enough to take the edge off.

Except I know the truth.

I'd never be satisfied with a quickie. I'd want more.

A sharp knock at my office door startles me. I straighten, forcing my expression into something neutral, expecting one of my staff members.

But it's not.

Finn's broad frame fills the doorway, the sight of him stealing the air from my lungs. The navy blue t-shirt stretches across his chest, hinting at the solid muscle beneath, while his cargo shorts sit low on his hips, drawing my attention exactly where it shouldn't go. His jaw is rough with scruff, and I can feel the phantom scrape of it against my skin.

"Maybe manifestation really does work," I murmur, a teasing smirk curving my lips.

"What makes you say that?" The intensity in his eyes is like a magnet, pulling me in, sending a pulse of heat straight between my legs.

I push out of my chair, crossing the small space toward him. "I was just thinking about you, and now here you are."

"What were you thinking about?"

"Technically, not *you*." My voice drops to something softer, something teasing. "More like your cock."

"Do you only like me for my cock?"

I shrug. "That… And your sperm."

He loops an arm around my waist and pulls me flush against him. "I should feel used."

"But you don't."

He slowly shakes his head, his gaze floating to my lips. "No, I don't."

And then he kisses me.

It's immediate, urgent, like he's been craving me just as much as I've been craving him. My fingers thread into his hair, tugging lightly as his hands slide lower, gripping my ass, forcing me against his hard length. A desperate sound escapes me, and he takes full advantage, deepening the kiss, capturing my breath, consuming me completely.

"I've always wanted to do this," he rasps, kicking the door shut behind him.

"What's that?" I pant as he buries his head in the crook of my neck, his unshaven jawline invigorating on my flesh.

"Bend you over your desk and fuck you."

A thrill shoots through me.

This is definitely getting out of hand.

And I should stop it.

But instead, I rise onto my toes and brush my lips against his. "Then what are you waiting for?"

With a growl, he slams his mouth back to

mine, our tongues tangling in a dance I feel all over my body. Too soon, he abruptly pulls out of the kiss and spins me around, bending me over the surface of my desk, papers and pens going flying.

"Good thing you're wearing this dress." He runs a hand up my leg, my muscles tightening as he nears the place I'm desperate to feel him. "I think we should add this to your list of rules."

"Add what?" I glance over my shoulder as he lowers his zipper, the heat in his stare almost too much.

"That you're required to wear a dress to work every day."

"Any reason for that?"

"So I can fuck you anytime I want." He pushes my panties to the side and brings his erection up to me.

When he thrusts into me, I have to fight back the scream begging to be set free. I'm already on dangerous ground here. The last thing I need is to bring even more attention to what I'm doing by screaming Finn's name.

"God, you're incredible," he grunts, his grip on my hips tightening as he drives in and out of me with an urgency I've never experienced. "You take my cock so damn good. I love watching me slide in and out of you. Seeing how wet you get for me. How greedy this pussy is for me."

"Finn," I moan, overwhelmed by his motions and words.

He smooths a hand along my backside, pushing the skirt of my dress up to my waist.

"It's made me think."

"What's that?" I ask, glancing over my shoulder once more and meeting his gaze.

"If your pussy is this greedy for me," he begins, sliding his hand over my flesh, "how would you react if I touched you here?"

He brings a hand to my clit. I'm about to remind him he's already touched me there countless times when he pulls his finger back and brings it up to the puckered flesh of my ass.

"Red or green?" he asks in a low, raspy voice.

My pulse increases, a million different thoughts filling me. No one's ever touched me there. But I want this. Want to experience everything I can with him.

"Green," I pant, my breathing ragged.

"Good girl," Finn praises as he slowly eases a finger inside, drawing a moan from me.

I try to stay quiet, but it's impossible with the unique sensations filling me. It's all too much, yet not enough.

"You should see yourself, Genevieve," he grunts, his motions increasing with desperation. "My cock fucking your pussy." He leans over me and bites my earlobe. "My finger fucking your ass."

I release a whimper, on the verge of shattering into thousands of pieces.

"You like that, don't you? Like me filling both your holes."

"God, yes."

"Before this is over, I'm going to take you here, too." He pushes his finger in and out of me with more urgency. "Can I do that? Can I fuck your ass?"

I'm so blissed out from sensation that I can barely put together a coherent thought. But the truth is, I want that with Finn. Want him to push me to my limits. Past my limits. Want to give myself over to him in every way possible.

Want him to *own* me in every way possible.

Except the one way that really matters.

"Yes," comes my garbled reply.

"What's that?"

"Yes, Finn. Yes, I want you to fuck my ass."

"And I will. When you're ready. For now, I want you to come all over my cock."

He doesn't have to ask twice. Between the relentless drives of his dick and the tempting circles of his finger, I'm putty in his hands, shockwaves rushing through me as I come undone around him.

"Fuck, Gen," he grunts as he picks up the pace. "Feeling your pussy and ass clench around me. My god. I've never felt this before. Never needed anyone as bad as I need you. Tell me you're mine."

"I'm yours," I exhale, my body consumed with tremors from the orgasm still ravaging me.

"Tell me this cunt is mine."

"My cunt is yours."

He circles my ass with his finger. "What about here?"

"It's yours, too. Every inch of me is yours, Finn. You own me."

"Oh, fuck," he exhales, his motions growing even more frenzied. Then he curves over me, his teeth clamping on my neck to muffle his cries as he jerks through his release.

Neither one of us moves for several long moments, the only sound in the office that of our ragged breathing.

Finally, he gradually pulls out of me, then helps me straighten. As he does, he presses his mouth against mine, his kiss soft and gentle, at complete odds with the way he just fucked me.

"Are you okay?" He cups my cheeks, forcing my eyes to his. "It wasn't too much, was it?"

A lazy grin crawls on my lips. "I gave you the green light." I hoist myself onto my toes, chasing his kiss. But before I can touch my mouth to his, he stops me.

"I just want to make sure you don't have any regrets."

"None." I bite my lower lip. "I like when you take

control. When you talk about using me. I probably shouldn't but—"

"Who says?"

A shrug is my only response.

"Listen to me, Gen." He tightens his grip on my face. "There's nothing wrong with having certain cravings or fantasies. I'm sorry you spent so much time with someone who made you feel there was. You won't get that with me. You want to give up control for a little while and explore these desires? I'm more than happy to give that to you." His mouth slowly descends toward me.

I pull him closer, giving serious consideration to the idea of taking the rest of the day off so we can go back to my place and explore even more of my fantasies.

But before I can suggest it, the alarm on my phone goes off, cutting the moment short.

"I need to go," I say with a groan. "I have a budget meeting at town hall."

"Don't let me keep you, then." Finn steps back, giving me space to adjust my dress.

I reach for a tissue, but he wraps a hand around my wrist, stopping me.

"Don't."

I furrow my brow, confused.

"I want you to go to that meeting with my scent all over you. With my come dripping from you, reminding you of where I was." He leans closer, his breath hot on my skin. "Reminding you that I own this pussy." He dips a finger under my dress, pushing my panties aside and teasing me. Then he glides it up my backside, toying with me there. "And this ass."

I moan, gently pulsing against him, desperate to feel him everywhere.

But he quickly releases me, making me long for his touch.

I take a minute to smooth my hair and adjust my dress, doing my best to look like I wasn't just thoroughly fucked by my best friend.

My best friend.

The words should be all the reminder I need to put some distance between us.

But all they do is send a shiver down my spine because, right now, Finn doesn't feel like my best friend. He feels like something else entirely. Something dangerous. Something I can't seem to quit.

Once I'm confident I look somewhat presentable, we step out of my office and into the library, Finn at my side.

I'm probably imagining it, but I swear every set of eyes drifts to us, as if they all somehow know exactly what we were doing behind my closed office door. It's irrational. My office is tucked away at the end of the administrative hallway, where only staff are allowed. There's no way anyone could know.

And yet, I feel exposed. As if what we're doing, what we've *been* doing, is written all over me.

When we finally step outside, I inhale deeply, letting the fresh air clear my head. Space. I need space from Finn. From this. From the way my body still hums in satisfaction while my mind screams at me to get a grip.

But I don't get my wish.

Before I can open my car door, Finn cages me against it, his body a wall of heat, his presence all-consuming.

"Can I see you tonight? Maybe bring Duke over so I don't have to worry about leaving early to feed him."

A voice in the back of my mind tells me I'm losing control of the situation. But Finn is a drug, and I'm already craving my next hit.

Besides, this could be our last month together. I may as well take advantage of it.

At least that's what I tell myself so I don't have to justify why I nod instead of tell him no.

"I'd like that."

I'm rewarded with his enigmatic grin, and he begins to retreat, giving me space to get into my car. But then he grabs my arm, tugging me back against him and capturing my mouth in a kiss.

I freeze.

Not because I don't want it. But because this is different.

Finn has kissed me plenty of times. But never like this. Never out in the open, in the middle of historic downtown, where anyone can see.

It's reckless.

It's dangerous.

It's everything I swore I wasn't going to let this become.

And yet, I don't push him away.

Because for one fleeting moment, I let myself pretend that Finn kissing me outside my place of employment isn't a risk. That it isn't a complication.

Instead, I pretend I could give him everything he needs. Everything he deserves.

Even if, in my heart, I know I never can.

an butter chicken and stirring the turmeric rice I made. The scent of warm spices clings to the air — cumin, coriander, ginger. It's nothing fancy, but she loves Indian food, so I wanted to surprise her with dinner after a long week of work.

The faint sound of a car door shutting outside sends a ripple of anticipation through me. I cover the pans and turn off the heat, my pulse kicking up in a way that makes no sense.

I see Genevieve every damn day. I've touched every inch of her skin. Memorized the sounds she makes when she's falling apart beneath me. Yet as the front door opens and she steps inside, it's like I'm seeing her for the first time.

She doesn't acknowledge me right away, too busy

toeing off her shoes and rolling her shoulders like she's shaking off the weight of the day. Her dress clings to her in a way that makes my throat go dry, the soft fabric draping over curves I've had beneath me, on top of me, wrapped around me.

It doesn't make sense, this hunger that coils deep inside me. I should've been satisfied by now. I shouldn't feel like it's getting worse. More desperate. More ravenous.

When Genevieve finally looks up and notices the dining room table is set, a far cry from our typical routine of eating on the couch or at the kitchen island, surprise flickers across her face, followed by a cautious, almost uncertain look.

"What's going on, Finn?"

I shrug. "I figured I'd give you the night off from cooking."

"You cooked?" Her eyes sweep over the table, taking in the details — the candles, the plates, the flowers I grabbed on my way over.

"Butter chicken with turmeric rice."

Her gaze snaps back to mine, and I can see the thoughts forming behind those deep, gray eyes. This isn't how we do things. This isn't part of the arrangement. This feels like something more.

She doesn't say it, though. Just offers a small smile and steps closer. "I thought you hated to cook."

"It's not my favorite thing to do," I confirm,

pouring some Cabernet Sauvignon into two glasses, handing her one. "But you're worth it."

My confession hangs heavy in the air, but before either of us can over examine it, she clears her throat.

"Do you need help with anything?"

"I have it all under control," I tell her, pulling a chair out for her. "You just relax while I plate everything."

She eyes me skeptically, but eventually sits down.

Once she's situated, I make my way back to the kitchen, carefully plating the rice and chicken before adding the small bowl of tomato and cucumber salad I'd prepared. Then I return to the table and set the plates down, the scent of butter chicken and warm spices filling the air as I take my seat across from her.

I know I did a damn good job. Dylan even said so when she tasted the sauce for me earlier after I begged her to come over and help. But now, as Genevieve picks up her fork, my palms are suddenly clammy.

I watch as she scoops up some rice, dragging it through the rich, red sauce before finally bringing it to her lips.

This is ridiculous. I've known this woman forever. Have seen her devour greasy diner burgers and sugary fair food. Have watched her close her eyes in bliss after the first sip of her morning coffee.

I tell myself I'm just curious to see if she actually likes it. That's all.

But the moment her lips close around the fork, it

feels like I'm waiting for the results of a test that could decide my future. I don't know why this moment feels so goddamn important. Why her approval, her enjoyment, means more to me than it should.

Finally, she lifts her gaze to mine, a small smile playing on the corner of her mouth.

"This is really good, Finn," she says, her voice soft with something I can't quite place.

And damn, it feels like I just won something.

Something big.

Something that should scare the hell out of me.

But when she takes another bite, her eyes fluttering closed in pleasure, the only thing I can think is that I want to see that look on her face again. And not just when she's eating my food.

"I'm glad you like it," I say in the hopes of thinking about something other than Genevieve's pleasure-filled moans. "I can't take full credit, though. I did have some help." I take a bite of chicken, savoring the combination of spices.

"Dylan?" she arches a brow.

"Who else?" I reach for my wine and swirl it around in the glass before bringing it up to my mouth, the robust Cabernet the perfect complement to the spice. "But she made me do everything myself. She just offered me some…guidance."

"Well…," Genevieve begins, dabbing at her mouth. Then she lifts her wine glass. "Here's to Dylan's guidance."

I clink my glass with hers, holding her gaze for several long moments, something shifting between us. Before it can build into something more, Genevieve tears her gaze from mine, refocusing her attention on her food.

"One thing's for certain. You'll make some woman very happy one day if you keep cooking like this."

I shouldn't be surprised by her remark. This is classic Genevieve. Whenever things get too serious or scary, she deflects. Puts up her walls.

A part of me wants to tell her she's the only woman I want to make happy. That I'm not doing this because it'll be good practice for a future relationship.

In truth, I'm not sure *why* I'm doing this.

Or maybe I don't want to admit why I'm doing this.

"Whatever happened to that girl?" she asks, swirling a piece of chicken through the sauce.

"What girl?" I frown, caught off guard.

"The girl you brought to my wedding? Hazel, or something?"

It takes me a second to place the name, but I eventually remember the woman she's talking about.

"I thought it was serious," she says, watching me carefully. "Weren't you talking about moving in together?"

"We were."

"What happened?"

I open my mouth, searching the recesses of my brain for an answer. For a moment, the memory is just out of reach, a shadow at the edges of my mind. I haven't thought about Hazel in years. Haven't thought about the night of her wedding in even longer.

But now that Genevieve has brought it up, the memories flash before me.

The hotel room was dimly lit, the glow from the San Francisco skyline spilling through the windows. Something about the night had drained me completely, left me hollow in a way I couldn't explain.

"Come to bed," Hazel murmured, leaning in to press a delicate kiss to my jaw while I continued to study the skyline as if it held all the answers.

"I'll be there soon." I took a long sip of my scotch, willing something to dull the ache inside me.

"Come on, Finn," she coaxed, stepping back and letting her silk robe fall away. "I'll make it worth your while.

I shifted my gaze to her, raking my eyes over her naked body.

I should have felt something. Desire. Excitement. The urge to sweep her up and lose myself in her.

Instead, my stomach twisted uncomfortably at the thought.

"I'm not in the mood tonight," I said, turning my eyes back to the city, the lights of the Bay Bridge twinkling in the distance.

A heavy silence settled in the room, and I could physically feel the heat of her glare scald my skin.

"It's her, isn't it?"

"What are you talking about?"

"Genevieve." Her name landed like a curse between us. "That's why you've been weird all night. Why you won't touch me."

"That's not—"

"Do you think I don't see the way you look at her? That you've always looked at her. And tonight?" She swallowed hard, her lower lip trembling. "All night, you couldn't take your eyes off her. You looked at her like—" She broke off, shaking her head.

"Like what?" I demanded, my jaw tight.

"Like you love her."

"She's my best friend."

She let out a sharp, disbelieving laugh. "Then why don't you ever look at me like that?"

I parted my lips, but no answer came.

Because I didn't have an answer for her.

She wiped at her eyes, her breathing uneven. "I'm not going to do this, Finn." Her voice was quieter now, resigned. "I'm not going to be the woman you settle for when you're in love with someone else."

"I'm not, Hazel. What do you want me to do to prove it?"

"Choose."

I stiffened, sucking in a sharp breath. "What do you mean?"

"Me or her. Who's it going to be?"

I never gave her a response. I didn't have to. She knew my answer without me saying a single word.

Hazel wasn't the first to accuse me of being in love with Genevieve. To make me choose.

And she wasn't the last.

One by one, I think back to every relationship I've ever had. The gradual retreats. The tearful accusations. The countless questions about my friendship with Genevieve.

The fights.

The ultimatums.

The choices.

And every single time, I chose Genevieve, even when she was married.

Not consciously.

Not deliberately.

But in the ways that mattered.

In the way my hands never lingered on another woman the way they do on her.

In the way no one else's laughter ever settled in my bones the way hers does.

In the way their kisses never brought me even a fraction of the hunger her mere touch always has.

And now as I watch her sip her wine, completely oblivious to the fact that she's holding my goddamn heart in her hands, it finally hits me.

I'm in love with my best friend.

TWENTY-SEVEN

Genevieve

Three months ago, I thought I had everything figured out. A plan. A goal. A clear, unemotional path toward motherhood that doesn't involve love or messy complications. Just Finn, my best friend and the person I trust more than anyone, helping me achieve this goal.

It should have felt strange. I should have felt absolutely nothing other than the friendship I always have.

That's not what happened.

Instead, being with Finn has been easy. *Too* easy.

Like slipping into something I was always meant to wear, only I spent years pretending it didn't fit.

Since Finn and I agreed to stop living by a calendar, I've stopped following the rigid rules that once defined my plan. No more tracking my cycle with militant precision. No more marking dates. No more restrictions on when to have sex.

Instead, Finn and I have enjoyed ourselves.

A lot.

Every time he touches me, every time we come together, it's felt so damn good that I haven't cared about the outcome anymore. The thing that once consumed me has faded into the background. The only thing that matters is him.

The way he grins at me before kissing me.

The way he touches me like I belong to him.

The way I feel more like myself than I have in years.

So much so that I wasn't even the least bit disappointed last month when I got my period. Because that meant another month of *this*.

Another month of Finn.

Which is why I was caught completely off guard when my mother texted me this morning, asking if I'd gotten my period.

I hadn't even noticed.

But when I did the math and realized I should have gotten my period five days ago, I knew I couldn't put it off any longer.

So I took a test. And another. And another.

Much like I did that first month in the hopes of getting a different outcome.

Now, as I stare at nearly a dozen positive pregnancy tests lined up on my bathroom counter, I'm not sure how to feel.

Happiness? Relief? Excitement?

This is what I wanted. The reason I started down this path.

So why do I feel a deep, aching sadness I don't know how to process?

A sharp knock at my front door startles me, jerking me from my spiraling thoughts, followed by my sister calling my name. Before I can think to hide the tests lining the counter, Claire peeks her head into the bathroom, her gaze landing almost immediately on the evidence spread across the surface.

She steps closer, completely ignoring me as she scans each test.

Each *positive* test.

"Oh, my god." Her eyes widen as she darts them to me, barely able to contain her enthusiasm. "You're pregnant?"

I swallow hard and nod. "I am."

She lets out a high-pitched squeal and lunges forward, wrapping me in a tight hug. "I'm so happy for you!"

Forcing a smile to my mouth, I weakly return her embrace, doing everything to fight back the rush of tears threatening to cascade down my cheeks, my throat tight.

"I can't wait to be an auntie." She beams as she

releases me. But her excitement dims when she rakes her gaze over me. "What's wrong?"

"Nothing," I say dismissively as I spin from her.

"Nothing?" Claire follows as I hurry into the kitchen. "You should be over the moon right now. Instead, you look like someone just told you your cat died." She glances at Holden as he bathes himself on the couch. "No offense, Holden."

My cat looks at her for a disinterested moment before returning to his grooming ritual.

"I'm just surprised, I guess. I didn't think it would happen this fast."

Claire narrows her eyes, studying me like she's peeling back layers I don't want exposed. "This is about Finn. Isn't it?"

"Of course not." I open the refrigerator and grab a bottle of water. "We had an agreement. That's it. Nothing more." I take a long sip of my water, purposefully avoiding her stare.

"Oh, please." She pushes out a disbelieving laugh. "If you ask me, it's a *lot* more than that.

"What are you talking about?"

She leans against the counter, crossing her arms. "You've been…different lately."

"Different?" I press, though I'm not sure I want to hear her answer.

"You've been lighter. Happier. And I have a feeling Finn has something to do with it, considering all the time you've been spending together."

"He's my best friend. We *always* spend time together."

She shakes her head. "Not like this. This is…more."

I swallow hard, unsure what to tell her.

While she knew Finn was helping me conceive, I never told her about the change to our agreement. That we've been sleeping together outside my ovulation window. That, over the past six weeks, I've had more sex than I had with Ethan during our six-year marriage. That I wake up beside him every morning, except when he's working. That every day at work, I count down the minutes until it's time to leave so I can lose myself in him.

Claire's gaze sharpens. "And I think that's why you're standing here looking like your world just ended instead of celebrating. Because in your mind, this isn't the beginning. It's the end."

"Claire, that's—"

"That's what this is really about," she interrupts, voice unwavering. "You're not upset because you're pregnant. You're upset because you're in love him."

My stomach lurches, and for a second, I think I might actually be sick.

"That's ridiculous." I force out a hollow laugh. "I love him as a friend. But I'm not *in* love with him."

"That's just what you tell yourself so you don't have to deal with what's actually happening."

A knot forms in my throat, but I swallow it down. "And what's actually happening?"

She leans in, her voice quiet but firm. "For the first time in your life, you let yourself have something because it feels good. You let yourself be happy. You let yourself *feel*. But now that it's real, now that there are stakes, you're terrified. So you're doing what you always do. Convincing yourself you never wanted it in the first place."

"That's not true."

"Yes, it is," she insists. "You push people away before they can leave you."

"Need I remind you, Ethan *left* me?"

"Maybe physically. But in reality, you were never truly *with* Ethan. He left because he didn't want to be with someone who never loved him. Who only chose him because she *wouldn't* love him. Tell me I'm wrong. Tell me the real reason you're standing here, refusing to admit your feelings, isn't because you're trying to protect yourself."

I part my lips, but no words come, my body physically resisting my denial. Instead, I say the only thing I can.

"We had an agreement."

Several tense seconds pass, the silence between us unnerving me. "You need to stop letting him control you, Gen," she finally says, her voice barely audible.

"Who? Ethan?"

"No. Dad. You're letting him control you. You've let him control you your entire life."

"No, I haven't. I—"

"Yes, you have!" She throws her hands up in exasperation, her green eyes flaming with frustration. "You never let yourself get fully invested in Ethan. You chose someone who was safe, someone who'd never wreck you if things went south. And when it did, you didn't even fight for it. You just accepted it, because it confirmed what you already believed. That nothing lasts."

I clench my jaw, each word she says cutting me harder and deeper.

"But Finn…" She draws in a deep breath, softening her tone. "Finn's different. And that scares you. Because you know if you let him in, *really* let him in, he could actually hurt you."

"You're making this into something it's not. Finn and me…" I shake my head. "It's not like that."

She studies me for a long moment, then sighs. "Maybe I am. Maybe I'm wrong about everything. It won't be the first time. But you need to ask yourself one thing… How much of your life have you spent trying to avoid becoming our father, only to turn out just like him anyway?"

"I'm *nothing* like him. I've never abandoned my family because I didn't want that life anymore."

"That may be true," Claire agrees. "But by running from anything that remotely resembles love, you're doing the same thing. If you keep pushing away the people who love you, someday you might end up just as alone."

I tighten my grip on the bottle, panic creeping in. I don't want to hear this. Don't want to think about this.

Because she's wrong.

She has to be wrong.

I'm *nothing* like my sorry excuse for a father.

And I'm *not* in love with my best friend.

TWENTY-EIGHT

Finn

I know something's wrong the second I walk into Genevieve's house.

She smiles as she greets me, but it's not the kind that makes her eyes light up.

It's the one you give when you're barely holding yourself together.

When you're terrified everything is about to fall apart.

"Hey," I say, pressing a kiss to her lips.

She lets me, but there's no heat behind it. No urgency. No need. It's brief, distant, like she's already slipping away.

Normally, the second I step through her door, she's on me, kissing me like I'm the air she needs to breathe. Tonight, she keeps her distance, crossing her arms and erecting a barrier between us.

A wall.

That single action sends a cold shiver of worry through me.

"Are you okay?" I rake my gaze over her frame, studying her demeanor.

When she hesitates, like she's about to tell me something important, my pulse immediately kicks up.

I try to do the math in my head. Since we stopped staring at a calendar, I haven't really kept track of her cycle. Could she be pregnant?

The idea doesn't just shake me. It fucking wrecks me.

Because somewhere along the way, this stopped being about a baby.

It became about her.

About us.

About the way I feel when I'm with her. The way she looks at me like I'm the only person in the world who truly sees her. The way my entire goddamn existence revolves around her, even if she doesn't realize it.

If she's pregnant, that means this arrangement has reached its expiration date.

Unless she wants more.

Unless she wants *me*.

I don't know if she does. She hasn't done anything to indicate she wants our arrangement to continue.

But she hasn't done anything to indicate she wants it to end, either.

This uncertainty is why I haven't told her how I feel. If I say it out loud, if I put my heart in her hands, she might not want it. She might insist this was all temporary, that I was only a means to an end.

If that happens, if I lose her completely, I don't think I can survive.

I convinced myself I'd rather have something than nothing at all. But now? I'm not so sure.

"Just had a rough day at work," she says finally, smoothing a piece of hair behind her ear. "The HVAC went out, so the library was sweltering. On top of that, some moms are making a fuss about certain books." She rolls her eyes. "Apparently, if a book includes characters that aren't white and straight, it automatically makes it obscene."

Her words are frustrated, but her tone is off.

There's something beneath the surface, something she's not saying. Maybe she really did have a shit day, but my gut tells me there's more to it.

"Anything I can do?" I ask.

A flicker of something crosses her face, but she shakes it off. "I just… I don't know. I need to get out of my own head."

I step closer, brushing my knuckles along her jaw. "Then let me help."

She hesitates again, but when I duck my head, kissing the soft skin beneath her ear, I feel her shiver.

"Helping you get out of your head is my specialty," I murmur, my lips skimming her throat. "Let me make you feel good."

"Finn." She grips my face, forcing my eyes to hers.

As she stares deep into my gaze, I get the feeling she's about to push me away. Give me the red light for the first time since we started sleeping together.

Then she slams her lips against mine.

Over the past several months, I've kissed this woman countless times. And each kiss has ignited something deep inside me. Something I didn't think possible.

But this kiss… This kiss feels different in a way that puts me on edge.

Genevieve pushes me down the hallway, her lips never leaving mine until we reach the bedroom. She tugs at my t-shirt, and I willingly let her rip it over my head, both of us frantically undressing like we're running out of time.

Once there's not a single scrape of fabric between us, I lower her onto the bed, my lips wandering along the contours of her body, desperate to taste every inch of her. But before I can, she stops me and forces me onto my back.

Without saying a single word, she wraps her fingers around my erection and straddles me. Her eyes remain locked on mine as she lowers herself onto me, enclosing me in her warmth.

Bliss washes over me, fire heating my veins. Not

just from the feel of her, but how damn beautiful she looks as she succumbs to her own desires.

She curves closer, her lips finding mine as she slowly circles her hips, her pace torturously slow. Normally, we go at it like animals, hard and fast, fucking each other until we're completely spent.

It's never been like this before. Never been filled with something I'm not quite sure how to describe. But I don't care about that right now. I stay in the moment with her, our eyes glued to each other as she sensually moves her body against mine.

I want to tell her how I feel. I want to say those three little words. Want to lay my heart bare and hope she doesn't shatter it.

But I don't.

Because if she doesn't feel the same, I won't just lose my best friend. I'll lose everything.

Instead, I hold on to her.

To this.

To the illusion that she's mine.

Even if it's only for tonight.

"Finn," she moans, increasing her motions, her body tightening around me, making it clear she's on the brink of falling over the edge.

As much as I want to prolong this, I'm powerless when it comes to Genevieve and her needs.

"Wait for me. I want to come with you."

She simply nods, holding my gaze as we chase our

bliss, both of us trembling and shaking through one of the most intense experiences of my life.

And when she collapses against me, her body warm and soft, I let myself believe that maybe she won't slip away.

That maybe I haven't already lost her.

But how can I lose something I never had to begin with?

TWENTY-NINE

Finn

I don't open my eyes right away.

A quiet, insistent voice warns that whatever today brings, I won't like it.

Especially after last night.

Instead, I inhale deeply, letting the faint scent of vanilla and something softer, something sweeter, something uniquely Genevieve, wrap around me like a memory I don't want to wake from. I reach across the bed, seeking warmth. Seeking her.

But I find nothing.

Cold sheets.

An empty space.

I glance at the clock, seeing it's after eight. She's probably already getting ready for work, like any other weekday.

Except today isn't like any other day.

I felt it last night. In the way she held on to me. In the way she let go.

Almost like she was letting go of me.

Of us.

Dragging a hand down my face, I shove away the unease curling in my stomach and pull on my t-shirt and shorts before heading to the kitchen. When I reach the doorway, I stop.

Genevieve's sitting at the island, her hands wrapped around a mug of tea. She's staring at something on the counter, her expression guarded, shoulders drawn tight.

At first, I can't tell what it is. But when I get closer, there's no mistaking it.

Even though I had a feeling this was the case, seeing the proof is still like a punch to the gut, my breath rushing from my lungs.

"Are you?" My voice comes out rough, not sounding like my own.

She lifts her gaze to me and swallows hard. Then she gives a small nod.

"I am."

I move without thinking, lifting her off the chair and into my arms. Regardless of what this means for us, emotion surges through me, raw and consuming. Pride. Wonder. Something so visceral I can't quite put a name on it.

She's carrying my child.

When we first made this arrangement, I told myself it wouldn't be a big deal. I had no plans to settle down, no burning desire to be a father. I was more than happy to give Genevieve what she wanted, to be the friend who helped her fulfill her dream.

That was before.

Before months of learning how she moves, how she tastes, how she feels.

Before falling asleep next to her every night.

Before realizing I want things I never thought I would.

And I want them with the one woman I'm not supposed to.

"I'm so happy for you," I murmur into her hair.

It's the truth. I'm beyond happy she's fulfilling this life-long dream.

But I'm also terrified.

Because I know what this is supposed to mean.

I just don't know if I can go back to the way things were.

If I can just forget about her.

If I can pretend these past few months didn't mean everything to me.

I hold her for as long as she lets me, dreading the moment she pulls away.

Because when she does, I might lose her completely.

And that thought? That possibility?

It's unbearable.

"I have to get to work." Genevieve presses against my chest after only a few seconds, gently pushing me back. I can practically see the wall she's already rebuilding brick by heavy brick.

"I'll walk you out."

"Thanks." She gives me a tight-lipped smile, then grabs her bag, leading the way outside.

When we reach her car, I open the door for her, but before she can climb in, I ask, "What's next?"

She faces me, adjusting the strap of her bag. "I have an appointment at the end of next week to confirm the pregnancy, but considering nearly a dozen tests were positive, I'd say it's just a formality."

"I'll go with you," I offer before I can stop myself.

"You don't have to," she responds with a harsh shake of her head.

"I know I don't have to." I step closer, lowering my voice. "I *want* to."

"Finn…" I hear the warning in her tone, but there's something raw beneath it. Something uncertain. "We had an agreement. You don't have any responsibilities to me. To either of us."

I open my mouth, ready to tell her I want more than that. That I want this to be something more than just an agreement. That I won't be happy watching her raise our child without being a part of his or her life. That I want everything. And I want it with her.

"Red light," she says before I can utter a syllable.

Her voice is barely a whisper, but it slams into me with the force of a goddamn wrecking ball.

"What?"

"I don't want you to say what I know you're going to. I can't give you what you're about to ask for."

I clench my jaw. "You don't even know what I was going to say."

"Yes, I do." She smiles sadly, her eyes glossing over. "I told you from the beginning. I want a child without needing to depend on someone else to raise them with me. Without having to worry about my child being abandoned."

"I'd never do that to you, Genevieve." My voice is determined, my heart hammering against my ribs. "I want—"

She holds up her hand, cutting me off. "That hasn't changed." She tries to sound firm, but her voice wobbles at the end. Then she wraps her arms around me, and I do what I always do. I hug her back. "Thank you for always being such an amazing friend."

Hearing her call me a friend cuts harder than I knew a single syllable could. My chest feels tight, like there's a vice around it, squeezing the air from me.

"And for giving me the greatest gift anyone could." She allows me to hold her for several more seconds before pulling back and releasing me. "Now, more than ever, I need my best friend. Like we agreed. Like you promised."

I stare at her, my throat burning, my hands clenching into fists.

There's so much I want to say. But will it make any difference? I know better than most how Genevieve is. Know why she feels like she needs to do this alone.

So instead of telling her those three words I've kept to myself, I force myself to give her space before I lose her forever.

"Drive safe," I say, my voice hollow.

She hesitates, like she wants to say something else.

Then she climbs into her car and drives away.

Taking my heart with her.

THIRTY

Genevieve

The drive to work is a blur.

I don't remember hitting the turn signal. Or stopping at red lights. Or pulling into the library parking lot.

All I can think about is the utter despair in Finn's expression when I pushed him away. Like I just cut the ground out from beneath him. Like I ripped something out of his chest with my bare hands.

I tell myself I did the right thing. That it would've been cruel to let him believe this could be more when I'm incapable of giving him that.

Knowing I did the right thing doesn't make it sting any less.

It doesn't make the ache in my chest go away when I think about climbing into bed alone tonight.

I've done it before. Every time Finn worked a twenty-four-hour shift. Every time he hung out with his brothers. Every time life happened.

But this is different.

Because I'll be alone when I could be with him.

That makes it so much worse.

The summer heat presses down on me as I make my way inside the library, but the second I walk through the doors, the warmth outside feels almost cool in comparison.

The library is sweltering, fans humming in a desperate attempt to circulate the air. The windows are open, but it doesn't help much. This old building traps heat like an oven.

When I approach the front desk, Taylor, one of my employees, looks up from the computer.

"Please tell me you heard from the HVAC company."

"They said a technician would be out sometime between ten and four."

I roll my eyes. "Of course they did."

Nothing like a six-hour window to keep me on my toes.

Aggravated but relieved that someone's at least coming, I head to my office and drop into my chair, the leather sticking to the backs of my thighs. I reach for my water bottle and take a sip, trying to focus on work.

But the moment I power up my computer, my mind returns to Finn.

To the way his voice cracked when he said my name.

To the way his eyes pleaded with me.

To the way I forced him to swallow whatever words he was about to say.

I quickly shake off the memory and focus my attention on my computer screen, blaming my lack of concentration on the heat.

Not because I can't help but wonder if I've made the biggest mistake of my life. If maybe Claire was on to something when she accused me of constantly running from love.

The idea consumes me all morning while I work on a proposal for a new literacy program until a knock sounds on my door a few hours later.

A part of me worries it's Finn stopping by with coffee. Instead, Taylor peeks her head in.

"The HVAC guy's here."

I push out a relieved breath. Finally some good news.

I rise from my chair, my skin peeling away from the leather, and step down the administrative hallway and into the lobby.

A man stands near the circulation desk with a clipboard in hand. He's broad-shouldered with a full head of gray hair, wearing a work shirt with the logo of an HVAC company. There's something familiar about him, but I shake it off. Everyone looks familiar in a small town.

"I'm Genevieve Thomas." I extend a hand. "The head librarian.

The moment I say my name, he does a double take. It's quick, barely there, but I notice his eyes widen slightly before he schools his expression.

Something uneasy shifts in my stomach, but I shove it down.

People recognize me all the time. Locals come in and out of the library, and my name is listed in half the town's event bulletins. Maybe he's just putting a face to it.

I show him around the library, making sure he and his crew have access to everything they need to fix the air conditioning. Then I return to my office and throw myself into my to-do list, determined to shake off the morning's events.

It doesn't work.

Finn lingers in the back of my mind like a phantom, an ache I can't ignore.

It's past one when Taylor knocks again. "They're finishing up," she says.

I head out to thank them, finding the same man from earlier waiting near the front desk.

"I appreciate you coming out," I say, accepting the paperwork he hands me.

His eyes flick over my face. Another too-long

glance. Another strange shift in his expression. "No problem."

He hesitates, like he wants to say something else. But then he just nods and leaves.

I watch him for several long moments, searching my brain for a memory. A spark. Something that tells me why I feel like I know him.

Nothing comes.

If my mother were here, she'd tell me I probably knew him in a past life.

Turning, I make my way back to my office, scanning the paperwork as I go.

But when I see the technician's name, I freeze.

Because it's not just any name.

It's my *father's* name.

Calvin Faulkner.

It's a coincidence. It has to be.

But the way he looked at me. The hesitation. The recognition.

Could it be him? Was that man my father? Did he know who I was? Is that why he acted that way?

I glance back toward the doors he just left through, contemplating going after him to ask, when a work truck bearing the logo of the HVAC company drives by.

"Everything okay?"

I snap my eyes toward Taylor, unsure what to say. "Better now that we have working air conditioning again."

"You're telling me."

I hurry the rest of the way into my office, pacing the short strip of carpet in front of my desk as I debate what to do.

I should forget about it. Forget about *him*.

But I need to know.

Grabbing my phone, I press my mother's contact before I can think clearly or talk myself out of it.

"Genevieve, darling," she answers as if she doesn't have a care in the world. "I hope you're calling to tell me I'm about to be a grandmother. Have you—"

"Where does Dad work?" I cut in sharply, a bitter edge slicing through my words.

A second passes. Then another. Finally, she sighs. "You don't need that energy in your life right now. Just focus on good things. Things that bring you joy," she says in that light, sing-song voice she uses when she's trying to steer me away from upsetting topics. "Is that what this is about? Because you're pregnant?"

I squeeze my eyes shut, feeling a stress headache coming on.

"I'll take a test tonight," I lie, not wanting to get into this right now.

"Oh, baby, that's so exciting. I have a feeling you already are. I felt phantom kicks this week."

I don't respond. I don't even know what to say to that. Instead, I do my best to redirect her to the reason for my phone call.

"Can you please just tell me what my father does for work?"

She sighs again, this time in frustration. "Gen—"

"Please, Mom. I need to know."

"I have no idea what he's doing now. I haven't spoken to him in over twenty years. You know that."

"What about before? What did he do for work before he left?"

There's a beat of silence. She must finally hear the desperation in my tone because she eventually says, "He was an HVAC technician."

My hand tightens around the phone as my gaze drops back to the work order, an icy chill racing down my spine.

It was him. He was standing right in front of me.

And he didn't say a damn thing.

THIRTY-ONE

Finn

The beer in front of me is warm. Has been for a while.

I should drink it. Should at least pretend I came here to unwind instead of sitting at the bar like some brooding asshole, staring at the amber liquid while my brain runs in circles.

But I can't.

All I can think about is Genevieve. The way she looked at me this morning, like she was bracing for impact. Like I was something she had to defend herself against. Like she was shutting the door before I even had a chance to walk through it.

That look gutted me, sent a slow, creeping ache through my chest that hasn't eased since. I've been trying to shake it, but hell if I know how. Instead, I pick up the glass and take a long swallow.

It doesn't dull the fact that, this morning, the woman I love told me, without saying the words, she doesn't want me.

The brewery is quiet this afternoon, a few regulars scattered across the tables while Jude moves in and out of the back, tending to the tanks.

Dylan's behind the bar, wiping down a stack of pint glasses, her sharp eyes cutting to me every few minutes. She's been watching me since I sat down, and I know her well enough to sense she's about to say something.

I'm right.

"You look like someone ran over your dog," she finally remarks, setting the last glass on the rack.

I huff a quiet laugh and shake my head. "Duke's just fine."

"But are you?" She leans toward me, dropping her voice. "Does this have something to do with Genevieve?"

I push out a long breath before meeting her gaze. "She's pregnant."

It's the first time I've said those words out loud.

Genevieve's pregnant.

The knowledge hits differently now.

Before, her pregnancy was an abstract thing. A decision born of logic. She wanted a baby, and I wanted to be the one to give her one. In my mind, it wasn't *my* baby.

But now?

Everything's changed.

It's not just *her* baby growing inside of her.

It's *my* child. A life we created together.

The realization wraps around my ribs like a steel vice. I should be happy. Thrilled. But all I feel is this gaping, hollow ache.

"How do you feel about this news?"

"Does it matter? I'm not supposed to care. I promised I wouldn't."

"But you do."

I draw in a slow breath and admit, "I do."

There are no teasing remarks. No boastful "I told you so." She just looks at me with genuine concern.

"Have you told her how you feel?"

"Not…exactly."

"Then why are you sitting here? Go tell her."

I take a large gulp of my beer. "I can't."

"Why?"

"Because she doesn't want me to."

"Wait. What? That doesn't make any sense."

I glance away, flexing my fingers against the smooth wood of the bar. "I started to tell her this morning, but she stopped me before I could even get the words out. Told me she can never give me what I was about to ask her."

Dylan doesn't answer right away, and when I

finally look back at her, she's studying me, her gaze sharper than before.

"Let me get this straight…" She plants her hands on the bar. "You were about to tell her how you feel, and she shut you down?"

I nod.

"And you just walked away with your tail between your legs?"

"What else was I supposed to do?"

Dylan exhales through her nose, shaking her head like I'm a lost cause. "God, men are idiots."

"Don't hold back. Tell me how you really feel." I take another long sip of my beer.

"Look, I get it. You and Genevieve have a history, and you're scared if you push too hard, she'll shut you out. That if you put it all out there and she doesn't feel the same way, you'll lose her altogether."

The words hit like a direct strike to my gut. That's exactly what I'm afraid of. What I've *been* afraid of since I realized I'm in love with her.

"Let me ask you this," Dylan continues, her tone softer now. "Do you really think you can go back to being friends? Be Uncle Finn to her kid? To *your* kid? Pretend this never happened?"

I open my mouth, but nothing comes out.

Because I don't know.

I don't know how to be in Genevieve's life without wanting more.

Without wanting everything.

Dylan watches me struggle, then shakes her head. "You can't, Finn. You'll be fooling yourselves. That will only make the inevitable worse when it finally blows up."

Something cracks open in my chest. Because deep down, I know she's right. Genevieve and I crossed that line and, despite our promise to each other, there's no way to go back. Not anymore. Not after everything we've shared.

"Do yourself a favor." Dylan straightens, pinning me with a look. "Tell her how you feel. To hell with whether it makes her uncomfortable. In fact, maybe that's what she needs so she'll finally admit her feelings for you. To be uncomfortable."

The idea of pushing Genevieve and losing her as a friend makes my stomach twist.

But haven't I already lost her? What do I have to lose by saying what I need to say? What I *deserve* to say. To hell with whether she wants to hear it.

I deserve the chance to tell her. Because if I don't, I'll regret it for the rest of my damn life. If losing my father taught me anything, it's to live life with no regrets. I've done precisely that since he died. I'm not about to stop now.

THIRTY-TWO

Genevieve

I can't stop shaking.

I thought I was past this. Thought I had healed, or at least learned how to live with the gaping hole in my chest where a father should have been.

But then he walked into the library today, and I was six years old again, my backpack straps cutting into my shoulders, my legs swinging off the edge of the porch. I can still picture that flickering streetlamp, just like on the day I waited for him to come home. Every set of headlights made my heart leap. Every car that passed somehow shattered it all over again.

And today when he looked at me, *really* looked at me, I saw it in his eyes. Recognition. He knew who I was and still walked away. Just like he did all those years ago.

A fresh wave of hurt crashes over me, suffocating and raw. I wrap my arms around myself and stare at the walls of my living room. I should call someone. Claire, maybe? But she wouldn't understand. She never knew him. Mom would listen, but what good would it do? She'd only tell me the same thing she has since he left. That he's not worth my tears.

I immediately think of Finn.

Any other day, he's exactly who I *would* call. He'd come over, no questions asked, and sit with me until the weight of everything didn't feel so crushing. But I can't keep leaning on him. I need to pull back. Redraw the lines we blurred.

So I stew. Alone.

As I stare at my phone, an idea pops into my head. I shouldn't do this. I've gone years without look-ing. But the need to know outweighs the warning bells going off.

My fingers move of their own accord as I navigate to a popular social media app and type the name that has haunted me my entire life into the search bar.

Calvin Faulkner.

A few results pop up and I scroll through them, somewhat relieved when they're not my father. But that relief is short-lived when I stumble across a familiar face. The same man who stood in front of me today and said nothing.

I should stop. Put my phone down and forget he ever stepped foot in my library. But I can't help myself. Can't help but be curious about the man who was supposed to love me. Who was supposed to cherish me. Who wasn't supposed to leave.

I click on his profile, finding it bare. A few shared links, nothing personal. Nothing to indicate what kind of man he is. Who he is now. Why he abandoned us.

Why he didn't love us.

Didn't love me.

I'm about to click off the screen when my thumb hits the app's home button out of habit, and suddenly, I'm staring at another picture. One I wasn't expecting.

Ethan.

My breath catches, a sharp inhale that feels like it gets stuck in my chest. It's been a while since I've seen his face and, for a second, I wonder if I'm imagining it. If maybe my mind conjured him up because I'm already feeling raw after seeing my father.

But there's no doubt in my mind. This is real.

Rebecca is beside him, her hand resting on his chest, her fingers curled like she belongs there. And nestled between them, wrapped in a soft pink blanket, is a baby.

Their baby.

Then I read the caption, the icing on an already shitty cake.

I never knew a love like this could exist until I became a father.

It shouldn't sting like this. After all, I'm pregnant. I'm going to be a mother. This was the goal. The dream. But seeing this photo rips something open inside of me.

A tear slips down my cheek, then another, until I'm gripping the phone with both hands, my breaths coming in ragged gasps.

Why wasn't I enough?

Why didn't he stay?

First my father. Then Ethan.

If I ever needed confirmation I did the right thing this morning with Finn, this is it. It's better I do this on my own. That way I don't come to depend on someone, only for them to leave.

Just like everyone else in my life.

Suddenly, the sound of the doorbell rips through the space, the surprising invasion causing me to nearly drop my phone.

I don't make any move to answer, in no mood to talk to anyone right now.

Then a familiar voice cuts through.

"Genevieve, it's me."

Shit.

Just my luck. During my lowest moment, Finn stops by to witness it.

"I know you're home," he calls through the door, knocking louder this time. "If you don't open up, I'm letting myself in. We need to talk."

I close my eyes, my fingers curling against my

palm. Damn him for having a code. Damn me for giving it to him.

Just as I stand to let him in, the lock beeps and the door swings open.

I barely have time to swipe at my wet cheeks before he's steps inside, his eyes immediately finding mine.

"What's wrong?" he asks, concern covering his expression. "Is it the baby?"

"No," I whisper, my voice hoarse. "The baby's fine."

Relief flickers over his face, but it's brief. "Then what is it? What's wrong?"

"Nothing. Just hormones, probably."

He doesn't buy it. "Genevieve." He closes the distance between us in three long strides.

I try to step back, but the coffee table stops me short. His hand comes up, gentle but firm, his fingers grazing down my arm, like he's trying to soothe whatever storm he can sense is raging inside me. Finn has always been my safe place, the one person who sees through me even when I don't want him to.

Right now, I *really* don't want him to.

"Talk to me," he says softly. "Please."

I stare at the spot on my arm where his fingers rest. His touch is warm, grounding. The weight of the day, the unbearable ache in my chest, it all comes crashing down until I can't hold it in anymore.

"My dad," I whisper. "I saw my dad today."

Finn goes still. His thumb pauses mid-stroke against my skin. "Your…dad?"

I nod.

On a long exhale, he wraps his arms around me. And I let him hold me. It's the one thing I don't want, but the one thing I need.

"What happened?" he asks after a beat.

"He was at the library," I say into his chest. "He was the HVAC repair guy. And he knew, Finn. He knew who I was and didn't say a damn thing." My voice cracks, and I hate it. Hate how weak it makes me sound, but I can't stop. "He just…*looked* at me. Like he was seeing a ghost. And then he walked away without saying a word. Without an explanation. Without a fucking apology."

Finn cups my cheek, forcing my gaze to his. His touch is so damn careful, like I might break apart in front of him. Maybe I will.

"He's not worth your tears, Genevieve." His voice is low, steady. "Don't give him that power."

I let out a shaky breath, pressing my lips together so they don't tremble. "And then—"

"Yes?" he prods.

"Then I saw Ethan."

"Where?" He frowns, his thumb catching a tear I didn't realize had fallen.

"Not in person. On social media. There was a photo." My stomach twists violently, bile rising in my throat. "Him. Rebecca. Their newborn daughter." I laugh, but it's a broken, brittle thing. "And the best part?" I drag in another breath, my entire body shaking now. "The caption. 'I never knew a love like this could exist until I became a father.'"

The words taste like acid on my tongue. Saying them out loud makes them real, makes the pain sharper, slicing through me all over again.

I don't realize I'm crying until Finn's arms are back around me, pulling me in, holding me together while I fall apart. I don't fight him. I can't. Not when the grief and loneliness are suffocating me, dragging me under.

"Why?" I whisper, my fingers fisting in his shirt. "Why wasn't I enough?"

"Don't," Finn demands, pinching my chin and dragging my eyes back to his. "Don't you dare say that."

"I just…" A sob rips through me, raw and unfiltered. "Why am I so unlovable?"

Finn pulls back just enough to cup my face in both hands. "You are *not* unlovable, Genevieve." His gaze is fierce, his thumbs brushing away my tears. "I love you."

The room tilts, and I swear the floor shifts beneath me. My pulse pounds in my ears, drowning out everything but those three words.

I love you.

My body locks up, my grip on his shirt tightening as if I can hold the moment still. Rewind it. Erase it.

He can't say this.

Not when my heart is already cracked wide open, bleeding out from wounds I don't know how to close.

I sensed he wanted more this morning, but I thought he just wanted to keep sleeping together. Maybe see if this thing between us might go somewhere.

I never expected he'd tell me this.

"As a friend. Right?" I ask softly, praying I misinterpreted him.

A serenity washes over his face, as if he didn't just turn my world upside down. "No. Not as a friend. I'm in love with you, Genevieve."

My breath hitches, panic clawing its way up my throat. Finn's hands are still on my face, his thumbs sweeping over my cheeks, erasing my tears.

"You don't mean that."

"I do." His voice is rough, strained, determined. "I'm so damn in love with you. Have been for years. It just took me this long to figure out what these feelings are."

"No," I exhale, shaking my head.

"You can act like you don't know it. Like you don't feel it, too. We both know you do."

"I... I can't do this." I manage to free myself from his hold, putting space between us. "You're not supposed to feel this way."

"You don't get to tell me how to feel, Genevieve."

"But you can't. You can't love me."

His brows draw together. "Why the hell not?"

I press a hand to my chest, trying to hold myself together. "You're my best friend. The only person who's never let me down, never left me." My heart squeezes painfully. "If I lose you, I lose everything."

Finn pushes out a long sigh as he steps toward me, reaching for my face again so I can see the truth in his words. "I'm not going anywhere."

"You don't know that," I whisper.

"Yes, I do." He adjusts his stance, bringing his body within a breath of mine. "You think I haven't imagined every way this could go wrong? I have, Genevieve. Every damn day. But as I've played through all these scenarios, I've learned something."

"What's that?"

"That the only thing worse than losing you would be never having you at all."

"Finn…"

"Don't push me away," he interjects before I can give him more excuses. "Don't do that to us."

"There is no us. There can't be." I push out of his hold, fighting to put space between us.

"There's *always* been an us, Genevieve. It just took me this long to finally realize it."

"No." I vehemently shake my head. "There isn't. Not like that. Not now. Not ever."

My words echo in the house, the seconds ticking by in a slow march. I see the hurt in his expression, but I can't take them back.

"Then say it, Genevieve." His strained voice breaks through the silence.

"Say what?"

"Say you don't love me. I need to hear you say it. Hear you say you haven't thought about this. That you're not dreading falling asleep alone tonight, wishing it was me in your bed instead of being surrounded by this empty fucking house."

His jaw is tight, his hands fisted at his sides, like he's bracing himself for impact.

"Say the last few months meant absolutely nothing to you. That *I* mean nothing to you. Say the words and I'll go, Genevieve. But I need you to tell me first."

I lick my lips, avoiding his gaze, hating what I see within. "Finn—"

"Say it." His voice cracks. "Look me in the eye and tell me you don't love me."

My throat burns. My insides twist into something awful. Something unbearable.

But all I can think about is the way my father looked right through me. The way Ethan held his newborn daughter, his entire world cradled in his arms while I stood on the outside looking in.

Finn is compassion and warmth and safety. He's everything I've ever wanted.

Which means he's the biggest risk of all.

I force myself to meet his gaze, even as my stomach clenches. Even as my hands tremble at my sides. Even as my throat fights against the words I'm about to say.

"I don't love you."

The silence that follows is deafening.

Finn's chest rises and falls with quick, sharp breaths, his jaw clenching so hard I swear I hear his teeth grind. Then he steps closer, his fiery eyes boring into mine.

"You're lying, Genevieve."

"I'm not."

"The hell you aren't. You think I don't know you? You think I don't see right through you?" He laughs, but there's no humor in it, just something wrecked and hollow. "You're scared, Genevieve. That's all this is. That's why you're doing this."

I swallow hard, but I keep my expression blank. I have to.

"You think I'm like every other man in your life," he says, his voice quieter now but just as fierce. "That I'll leave. That I'll disappoint you. That loving me is a mistake. But I'm not them." He takes another step forward. "And I'm sure as hell not giving up on you just because you're too scared to admit you love me.

"You don't get to push me away and expect me to just take it. I know what this is, and I know you. I'm not giving up on you, Genevieve. Not like every other man in your life has. I'll give you the space you obviously need to process this and get your head on straight. But this isn't over. *We* aren't over."

Then he turns and storms out of the house, the door slamming shut behind him.

I stand there, frozen, my pulse hammering, my chest caving in on itself.

The silence is deafening, the emptiness unbearable.

And for the first time in my life, I feel completely, utterly alone.

THIRTY-THREE

Finn

The scent of freshly brewed coffee wraps around me as I push through the doors of the coffee shop, like I do every Monday morning. The rich aroma used to be comforting, a familiar part of my routine. Today, it reminds me that something is missing.

The barista behind the counter, a college-aged blonde with a tired smile, perks up when she sees me.

"The usual, Finn? Two Americanos, one black, one with two percent?"

I shake my head. "Not today. Swap the two percent for a ginger tea."

Her brows lift slightly, but she doesn't ask questions as she rings me up. I slide a bill across the counter and step to the side to wait for my order.

Genevieve can try to push me away all she wants. She can deny her feelings, pretend what we shared means nothing. But I'm not like her father. I'm not like Ethan. I'm not going anywhere.

I'll wait as long as it takes for her to realize that.

The barista calls my name, and I grab the two cups, the warmth seeping into my fingers as I step outside.

It's a short walk to the library, and the town is already waking up — shopkeepers flipping over their "closed" signs, a couple of early risers walking their dogs. This place has always felt steady. Unchanging. But today, I feel off balance, like I'm moving through a version of my life where something — some*one* — is just out of reach.

When I enter the library, the quiet swallows me. The smell of old books and polished wood lingers in the air, familiar and grounding.

At the circulation desk, Taylor looks up from her computer and smiles. "You're early today. Genevieve's not in yet."

"Just wanted to drop this off for her before heading to the fire station." I hold up the cup. "Should I leave it with you?"

"You can take it to her office. Her hands are always full when she comes in."

"Thanks."

"Of course."

I head toward the administrative wing, the sound

of my shoes muted against the carpet. Genevieve's office is exactly the same as it's always been, but being here without her feels different. The room smells like her — warm vanilla and soft flowers, with a faint hint of aged pages — and it makes me miss her even more.

I set the tea on her desk and pull the small bag of hard candies from my pocket, placing it beside the cup. Then I grab a notepad and jot down a quick note:

> *I took the liberty of changing your order to a ginger tea (it's caffeine-free). I also read hard candies are good for morning sickness.*

I hesitate for a second, then write the last part.

> *Love,*
> *Finn*

The words sit there, staring back at me. My fingers twitch to cross them out, to soften them somehow. But I don't.

She can ignore them. Pretend she didn't see them.

But I won't pretend I don't mean them.

Folding the note, I place it underneath her tea. Then I turn and head to the firehouse, hoping work will distract me from thinking about Genevieve.

But nothing does.

Instead, I find myself checking the clock every few minutes, wondering if she's at the library.

And if she is, why haven't I heard from her?

I didn't expect her to drop everything and declare her love for me after leaving her a tea and some hard candies. But I hoped for *something*.

Not the continued radio silence that's plagued our relationship for the past week.

"Jesus, man," Murphy snorts, pulling me out of my thoughts. "You waiting for a hot date?"

"What are you talking about?"

"You keep looking at your phone like you're expecting it to ring." He stretches out in his chair, crossing his legs at the ankles. "Hasn't buzzed once, by the way."

"It's nothing," I lie.

Which he picks up on easily. Of course he does. We may work together, but being in this profession, he's more like a brother than anything, considering the hours we spend together any given week.

And the fact we depend on each other to stay alive.

"I haven't seen Genevieve around much lately," he remarks after a beat. "You two have a lovers spat or something?"

"She's been busy. And we don't have lovers spats. She's just a friend."

They're words I've said to him dozens of times, but for the first time, they feel wrong. Because I don't want to be just friends with Genevieve. Not anymore.

And I have a feeling Murphy already senses that, considering he responds by shaking his head with an amused chuckle.

I'm about to re-iterate my argument, but am cut off by my phone buzzing on the table.

I grab it, relieved when I see Genevieve's name. *Finally.*

I swipe the message open.

GENEVIEVE:

Thank you.

Two words. But they're the first ones she's said to me in over a week. Even if it's just through a text, it's better than nothing.

I type back quickly.

ME:

You're welcome.

And then I wait.

The air in the waiting room is thick with the sterile scent of antiseptic and something vaguely floral, the kind of artificial fragrance meant to be soothing but only makes me more on edge than I already am. A stack of magazines sits on the table beside me, but I don't pick one up. I can't pretend to be interested in anything other than the reason I'm here.

I shouldn't be here. I know that.

Genevieve made her wishes clear, and I promised I wouldn't interfere. But I'm not only here because I'm the father of her child.

I'm here because I can't *not* be.

Because every day that's passed without seeing her, without hearing her voice, has felt like I've lost something I didn't even realize I couldn't live without.

I shift in the chair, my knee bouncing with restless energy. A pregnant woman across from me glances up from her phone, her eyes flicking to my leg. I force myself to still, and exhale slowly, dragging a hand over my jaw.

The clock on the wall ticks on.

Every second feels like an eternity as I anxiously wait for Genevieve to walk through those doors. I can already picture the look on her face when she sees me. The shock. The confusion. Maybe even a flash of something sharper. Annoyance. Resentment.

Despite any negative reaction, I knew I'd regret it if I wasn't here, even if I'm relegated to the waiting room. So I reached out to Claire.

I half-expected for her to insist that if Genevieve wanted me here, she would have told me herself.

That's not what happened.

Claire didn't hesitate to give me all the details. She even agreed to tell Genevieve something came up at work preventing her from coming so she might let me be a part of it.

Not that I think for a second she actually will.

She'll probably take one look at me and proceed to ignore me, just like she mostly has since I poured my heart out to her.

But I have to try. I don't care how long it takes for her to finally realize I'm not Ethan or her father. I'm not abandoning her.

And not just because she's carrying my child.

But because I can't imagine my life without her.

So I'll wait.

Suddenly, the door swings open and my pulse kicks up as Genevieve steps in. Her gray eyes lock onto mine, and she freezes in the doorway as the air shifts and thickens. Like the room is suddenly too small.

She gapes at me, her fingers curling around the strap of her purse, her lips parting on a silent inhale as she stares at me in confusion.

I take her in, my gaze sweeping over her like I'm seeing her for the first time.

Her dark hair is pulled into a low knot instead of spilling over her shoulders in gentle waves. Her frame is still tall and slender, but there's something different about the way she holds herself. A subtle shift in the way she stands. Maybe I'm imagining it, or maybe I'm just searching for some sign of the life growing inside her.

There isn't one. Not yet. But she's softer somehow, her features a little more tired, her lips pressed together like she's holding something back.

And fuck, I've missed her.

It's only been two weeks, but it might as well have been a lifetime.

I went from seeing her nearly every day to nothing. No small smiles from across the kitchen as we cooked together. No conversations that stretched late into the night. No laughter. No teasing. No Genevieve.

But now she's here, and I have no idea what to do or say. I didn't exactly think past being here for her.

Instead, all I can do is hold her gaze and hope I haven't made things worse.

THIRTY-FOUR

Genevieve

I blink, certain I'm imagining this.

It's one thing for Finn to mow my lawn. To leave my favorite tea on my desk. To find subtle ways to remind me he's still here. Still thinking of me.

It's another for him to be in the waiting room of my doctor's office.

I should be angry. I made him promise he wouldn't interfere with my pregnancy. That he wouldn't try to undertake any sort of fatherly role.

But as I take in the broad set of his shoulders, the way his t-shirt stretches over the solid lines of his chest, I can't summon the fury I wish I felt.

All I do feel is the rush of something warm and comforting.

I've spent the last two weeks convincing myself

any feelings I may have had were a byproduct of hormones. That the ache consuming every inch of me was nothing more than my body changing.

But now, standing here, looking at him... I was wrong.

His face is the same, yet different. Handsome, as always, but there's something missing. The spark that's always lived in his eyes is dimmed. Shadows cling to him, and I know without asking I put them there. The weight of that knowledge presses against my chest, hot and unbearable.

I drag in a breath and force myself to move toward the desk, trying to ignore the hammering in my chest.

The receptionist offers me a warm smile, and I tell her my name. She checks me in, then hands me a clipboard with a few papers on it. "Just fill these out, and we'll call you back in a few minutes."

I turn, and my gaze inevitably finds Finn's again. He's still watching me, his expression unreadable. Against my better judgment, I make my way toward him.

As I lower myself into the chair beside him, his scent wraps around me. That familiar mix of soap and cedar and something distinctly him. For a moment, I want to lean in, let it settle deep into my bones. But I don't. Instead, I grip the pen tighter and focus on the paperwork, refusing to acknowledge the way my pulse thrums with awareness.

Silence stretches between us, thick with everything unsaid, his mere presence making it impossible for me to focus.

When I'm not sure how much longer I can handle the uneasy tension between us, Finn's voice cuts through.

"How are you feeling?"

The simple question nearly undoes me. I forgot how much I missed the sound of his voice. The way it comforts me like a safety net.

"Okay," I respond evenly, forcing myself to keep my eyes on the papers in front of me. "I thought I'd have more time before morning sickness kicked in. Apparently not."

"Is it bad?" he asks, the concern in his tone evident.

I still don't look at him. I can't. If I do, I might break.

"I can keep food down, but I have no interest in eating. Except for those hard candies. I've been going through them like crazy."

"I'll get you some more," he says softly.

"You don't have to."

"I know. I want to."

I pin him with a glare. "You can't keep doing this, Finn," I hiss under my breath.

"What? Being your friend?"

"That's not what you're doing, and you know it. I

told you in the beginning I wanted to do this alone. I don't need anyone."

"I just want to be here for you. Be present. Nothing more."

I search his face, looking for deception. For some hidden agenda. There's nothing except raw, unfiltered honesty.

Before I can respond, a nurse calls my name.

I leap to my feet, grateful for the escape.

"Would you like anyone to join you?" she asks, her gaze floating to Finn before landing back on me.

I glance at him, hope flickering in his eyes. He wants me to say yes. Wants to be there.

But I can't do this. I can't let him in. I started down this path fully prepared to do everything alone. A few weeks of amazing sex hasn't changed that.

Forcing a smile to my lips, I return my attention to the nurse. "I'm fine on my own."

"Of course." I could be wrong, but it looks like she almost gives Finn an apologetic smile before returning her attention to me. "This way."

The exam room is cold, the flimsy gown like sand paper against my skin. But despite the excitement of this new adventure I'm about to embark on, my thoughts are elsewhere.

With Finn.

No wonder my blood pressure was slightly elevated.

The doctor enters, offering a warm smile as she congratulates me on my pregnancy.

We go through my medical history, discussing risks and expectations. Then she asks me to lie back so she can check on the baby. The nurse wheels the ultrasound machine closer and it whirs to life, humming softly. The seconds stretch as I stare at the screen. Finally, there's a flicker. A tiny, unmistakable shape.

My baby.

Except it's not just mine. It's *ours*. Finn's and mine.

The thought steals the air from my lungs.

It wasn't supposed to be ours. It was supposed to be mine alone. Something I fought for.

But so did Finn. He didn't have to offer to help me, but he did. Put his own life on hold to give me this gift.

And I have no idea how to feel about that.

Emotion swells in my throat, thick and consuming. My doctor hands me a printout, and before I can think better of it, I ask for another copy.

She nods and gives me the extra print.

I dress quickly and return to the waiting room. Unsurprisingly, Finn is still here. He doesn't speak as I pass him, but I can feel him. His presence. His patience.

He follows me outside, keeping a respectful distance as I walk across the parking lot.

When I reach my car, I hesitate, my fingers curled on the handle. Without giving myself time to change my mind, I pull the black-and-white photo from my purse. Then I turn and extend it toward him.

"Thought you'd like to have this."

He takes it from me, his throat bobbing as he stares at the image. "Is that…?"

"It is."

A quiet breath shudders out of him, his fingers tracing over the tiny shape. "Little bean." When he returns his gaze to mine, his expression is raw and filled with something I can't name.

Something I'm too scared to name.

"Thank you. For this. It means a lot."

I nod, swallowing against the emotion clawing up my throat. It takes everything I possess not to fling my arms around him and pull him against me. To lose myself in his warmth. His presence.

His love.

Before I can, I slide into my car and drive away.

It's not until I'm halfway back to the library that I finally remember to breathe.

THIRTY-FIVE

Genevieve

The GPS leads me through a neighborhood lined with cracked sidewalks and sagging fences, the kind of place that makes me grateful for the quiet familiarity of Sycamore Falls. Here, on the outskirts of Reno, the air feels heavier, thick with regret and memories that don't belong to me but somehow still weigh me down.

With every turn, doubt gnaws at me. Maybe this is a terrible idea. Maybe I should have told someone where I was going. Maybe some doors are better left closed. This is definitely one of my more impulsive decisions, one made during a moment of stubborn determination.

I'm not sure what I hope to get out of it. Closure,

maybe. Or confirmation that I'm doing the right thing by keeping my distance from Finn.

A few minutes later, I pull up to the address the private investigator gave me. I wasn't sure what I expected. Something empty and forgotten, like how I felt when he left.

And that's exactly what the single-story house looks like. The lawn is overgrown, the paint peeling, the front yard littered with cigarette butts.

I grip the steering wheel, my fingers pressing into the worn leather.

I should turn around. Forget I ever came here.

Forget *him*.

But I can't. I need to do this. For myself.

I open the car door and step onto the cracked pavement on unsteady legs. Each step along the weed-choked pathway feels heavier than the last. When I reach the front door, my pulse skyrockets and I hesitate, my knuckles hovering over the faded wood. Before I can stop myself, I knock and hold my breath, only to be met with silence.

Maybe it's a blessing in disguise. A sign I'm not meant to be here. Not meant to do this.

Just when I'm about to retreat, the door swings open, and I'm face-to-face with the same man who came to fix the HVAC at the library.

My father.

Air lodges in my throat as I stare at him, unsure what to say.

What do you say to the man who disappeared from your life when you were six? Who became a ghost?

"Can I help you?" he asks somewhat guardedly. Recognition flickers in his gaze, yet there's no warmth. No relief.

No love.

"My name's Genevieve Thomas," I finally say, my voice steady, even as my stomach twists. "We met at the library."

"I remember."

"I'm sorry for barging in on you like this. I just…" I blow out a shaky breath. "I have to know."

His expression shifts, and he rubs a hand over his stubbled jaw. "You want to know if I know who you are… Other than the librarian."

I square my shoulders, trying to exude confidence, despite feeling small. "Yes."

A painful silence settles between us as I lock my eyes on his. On eyes that look exactly like mine. I always wondered where I got mine from. Claire has my mother's shade of green. I'm the only one with the purple-gray hue.

Now I know, because the shade and shape of my eyes are an exact match to his.

Finally, he pushes out a long sigh and steps back, holding the door open. "You want to come in?"

Every cell in my body warns against this. But I walk inside anyway.

The scent of stale beer and fried food lingers in the air. The walls are lined with mounted deer heads, fishing trophies, and framed pictures of hunting trips.

But there are no family photos.

No evidence he ever had daughters.

No sign we ever existed.

Something in my chest tightens. I don't know what I expected. Maybe some proof he missed us. That he cared. That leaving was hard for him. That he's regretted it every day since.

But there's nothing other than his love of his hobbies.

"You're Judy's kid," he cuts through, yanking me out of my thoughts.

His statement is like a slap. A punch to the gut.

Not *my* kid. *Judy's* kid. Like I was never his. Like his DNA doesn't run through me.

I swallow against the sudden lump in my throat, forcing myself to stand taller. "I'm *your* kid, too."

He lets out a short, humorless laugh. "You don't look like a kid to me."

"I'm still your offspring," I retort, my voice sharper now. "I'm still half of you, in case you've forgotten."

He shifts his weight, obviously uncomfortable with my sudden reappearance in his life. "What do you want me to say?"

"I want to know why." The words spill out before

I can stop them, my pulse a frantic beat beneath my skin. "You had a family. And you just…walked away?"

His exhale is long and slow. "It wasn't about you."

"Not about me?" A cold, sharp laugh bubbles up from my throat. "You abandoned your family. You abandoned *me*."

"I had my reasons." His eyes flicker toward the door, like he's already planning his escape.

I step closer, not letting him avoid me like he has most of my life. "Then tell me what those were, because I've spent years trying to figure them out. I thought maybe if I was good enough, if I kept my room spotless, if I got straight A's, if I never caused problems, you'd come back. You'd realize I was worth staying for." My voice cracks, but I push through. "But you didn't. And now you're standing here telling me it wasn't about me? Do you have any idea how much easier it would have been if I could have believed that? Every single day, I watched other kids with their dads and wondered what made them special. What made them better than me. But you… You didn't even try."

He shrugs like it's no big deal. Like that one decision had no impact on anyone. "Your mom and me… We weren't good together. It was easier this way."

His statement slams into me, knocking the breath from my lungs.

It was *easier*.

I've said the same thing myself dozens of times.

I married Ethan because I thought it would be *easier* than risking my heart on real love.

I decided to have a baby on my own because I thought it would be *easier* than trusting someone to stay.

I pushed Finn away because I thought it would be *easier* than admitting the truth.

But as I stand here, staring at a man who has spent his whole life choosing easy, I see it for what it really is.

This isn't easy. This is *empty*.

A house filled with trophies, not people. A life measured in taxidermy and fishing trips, not love. A man alone because it was easier to walk away than stay and fight.

Is this my future?

Is this what I've been running toward?

I've repeatedly told myself it's easier to keep people at a distance. That love doesn't last. That if I never rely on anyone, I'll never be hurt the way this man hurt me.

But I now realize it was merely a lie I said to make myself feel better.

The real risk isn't loving someone.

It's waking up one day and realizing I let something real slip through my fingers because I was too afraid to fight for it.

I'm not going to do that anymore.

I'm not going to turn into this man.

I'm not going to take the *easy* way. Not anymore.

Squaring my shoulders, I level him with a stare. "I'd take real over easy any day."

Then I turn and walk away, leaving him and the lie I've been telling myself behind.

THIRTY-SIX

Finn

The radio crackles in my ear as the engine tears through the quiet streets, sirens screaming into the night. Inside the cab, no one speaks. We're all in the zone, mentally preparing for whatever awaits us on the other end of this call.

It doesn't matter how many times I've done this. Every time we roll up on a fire, there's a small, unspoken question hanging in the back of my mind: Is this the one that takes me out?

I shove that thought away, replacing it with something better. Something that grounds me.

Genevieve.

Little Bean.

The black-and-white ultrasound photo she gave me is still hanging on my fridge. I've memorized every blurred detail, tracing it with my eyes until I could practically feel the tiny heartbeat pulsing through the image.

My kid.

It still doesn't feel real. Not entirely. But in the quiet moments of my day, the reality of it sinks in. I'm going to be a dad.

A month ago, the idea wouldn't have carried the same kind of weight. But now? Now it's everything.

The engine screeches to a halt, forcing me out of my thoughts. We're already moving before the truck fully stops, spilling out with muscle memory precision.

Flames devour the house, shooting out of the roof in violent bursts, thick black smoke rolling toward the sky. The heat pulses, searing against my gear, but I barely register it.

"We've got an active fire on the first and second floors," Cappy's voice comes through the comm unit, assessing the scene fast.

Suddenly, a woman's scream cuts through the crackle and roar of the fire. "Please! My daughter! She's still inside. Her bedroom's on the second floor. First door to the right."

The words slam into me, quick and sharp.

A child.

Cappy doesn't hesitate. "Murphy. Lawrence. You know what to do. Primary search on the second floor. Get in. Get the kid. Get out."

We nod, pulling down our masks.

"Let's move," Murphy says, and we hurry up to the house, knowing full well that every moment counts.

The second we breach the front door, the fire is alive around us, roaring, licking at the walls. My mask and tank allow me to breathe through the smoke filling the space, but the heat is relentless.

Murphy secures a thin yellow rope to the front door, and I follow him into the house and toward the winding staircase.

"The stairs are holding," Murphy says, testing the first step. "For now."

"Make it quick," Cappy warns over the radio.

We take the stairs fast, low to the ground, hugging the wall. The fire snaps and growls above us, chewing through the ceiling, but we press forward.

The second-floor hallway is thick with smoke, but we don't retreat, moving to the first door on the right.

It's closed. A good sign.

Murphy pushes it open, and I scan the smoke-filled room. My flashlight cuts through the haze, searching for some sign of life. But I don't immediately see anything. I'm about to ask Cappy to verify the girl's room with the mother when I finally see it.

A shape curled in the corner, small and unmoving.

She's clutching a stuffed bunny to her chest, her tiny body trembling, soot smearing her tear-streaked cheeks. Wide, terrified eyes lock onto mine, and relief slams into me.

"I've got visual," I announce over the radio, eating up the distance and lowering myself in front of her.

"Hey, sweetheart," I practically shout so she can hear me through my mask. "I'm going to take you to your mom, okay?"

She doesn't move, frozen in fear.

The fire outside the room roars louder, embers curling inside. Time is running out.

I grab a blanket from the bed and wrap it around her, shielding her from the worst of the smoke. When I scoop her into my arms, she lets out the tiniest whimper and clings to my jacket with trembling fingers.

She's so damn small.

Something tightens in my chest, hard and unrelenting.

In a few months, I'll have a child of my own. A life I'll be responsible for.

Even if Genevieve decides she doesn't want me.

Even if she thinks she can do this alone.

I'll still be Little Bean's dad. And I'll still do whatever it takes to keep him or her safe.

"Finn, let's go!" Murphy calls out from the doorway.

I secure the little girl against my chest and move, keeping my steps controlled. The flames in the hallway are closing in, heat lapping at my back as we push toward the stairs.

Murphy goes first, testing each step and clearing a safe path for us.

The structure groans beneath us. Then a sickening crack reverberates in the space and the stair disappears beneath me.

Pain explodes through my leg as I plunge downward, my foot punching straight through the charred wood, sharp stabs of agony ripping up my calf.

I bite back a yell, forcing my arms to stay locked tight around the little girl. She lets out a tiny cry, burying her face into my jacket.

Panic flares. Not for me. For the little girl in my arms.

"Finn!" Murphy lunges, grabbing my shoulder before I pitch forward.

"Take her." I shove the girl toward him. "Get her out of here."

He hesitates, obviously not wanting to leave me behind. But getting this child to safety is our priority. He pulls her from my arms, wrapping her close.

"I'll be back for you." He disappears down the stairs, and I force myself to breathe through the searing pain in my leg.

My hands claw at the jagged wood, yanking, twisting, trying to free myself, but my boot is trapped in something solid beneath the floor.

I've always understood the risks of this job. But for the first time, I feel them in my bones.

What if one day, my kid is the one waiting for

someone to come home? What if they grow up without me, like I did after my dad died?

Like Genevieve did after her father abandoned her?

The thought is unbearable, but I try to push it down and focus on remaining calm.

"I'm coming back, Finn," Murphy says over the comm unit. "Hang tight."

"Thanks, brother," I reply, relieved.

The house moans around me, the sound deep and splintering.

Then an ominous groan echoes above me.

I snap my head up, watching as the ceiling above me buckles.

For a fraction of a second, time slows. Smoke churns, the orange glow above shifting.

Then it all comes crashing down.

THIRTY-SEVEN

Genevieve

My hands tremble as I shove through the hospital doors, my breaths coming in sharp, uneven gasps. The waiting room is a blur of sterile white walls, flickering fluorescent lights, and murmuring voices, but I don't register any of it.

I don't see faces.

I don't hear the noise.

All I can think about is Finn.

I need to see him. I need to know he's okay.

I was on my way to the station, finally ready to tell him the truth. To admit I don't want to go through this alone. That I want him in my life. Not just as my best friend. Not just as the father of my child. As mine.

But before I could get there, my phone rang.

When I saw Murphy's name on the caller ID, I knew something was wrong. I was right.

A fire.

A child rescued.

Finn in the hospital.

I don't even remember the drive here. Just the suffocating panic. The cold sweat clinging to my skin. The absolute certainty that if I lose Finn, there wouldn't be enough air in the world to keep me breathing.

I rush to the front desk, my pulse thundering in my ears. "Excuse me," I rasp to the nurse, barely recognizing my own voice. "Finnegan Lawrence. Where is he?"

She barely looks up from her computer. "Are you family?"

I hesitate, my breath hitching.

I don't have the title that gives me automatic access. I'm not his wife. Not his girlfriend.

But I'm carrying his child. And in every way that counts, he's mine.

"He's the father of my baby," I choke out. "Please. I need to see him."

She finally looks up, her expression softening, but not enough. "I'm sorry. I can't release patient information unless you're immediate family."

The words are a punch to the gut. I clutch the edge of the counter, frustration clawing up my throat like acid. "Please, I just—"

"Genevieve?"

The deep, familiar voice cuts through my panic. I whirl around, and relief crashes through me.

Finn's oldest brother stands a few feet away, his suit crisp, hair neatly groomed. At complete odds with my appearance. His sharp gaze takes me in — my frantic eyes, the way I'm practically vibrating with anxiety, the tears streaming down my cheeks.

I don't even care whether he overheard me say I'm carrying Finn's child. That's the least of my worries right now.

"She's with me," Hayden tells the nurse, his voice firm. Then he refocuses his attention on me, his tone softer. "Come on, Gen."

I follow him out of the waiting area and down the maze of hallways, a thousand thoughts fighting for attention.

"He's okay," Hayden assures me almost immediately, as if he senses I'm barely hanging on. "Stable. Took in some smoke, but his vitals are good. His leg is broken from when the stairs collapsed, and he has a mild concussion. But all things considered, he's lucky that's the worst of it."

"The stairs collapsed?" My voice wavers.

Hayden nods. "From what Murphy shared, they went in to rescue a little girl stuck in the house. On the way out, the stairs gave way. Finn managed to hand her off to Murphy. While he waited for his own rescue, the ceiling started to weaken. But Murphy and one of the other guys were able to free him just before the entire roof caved in."

"Is he awake?" I ask.

"He sure is. He's in a bit of pain, but he lives to fight another day." Hayden gives me a reassuring smile as we stop in front of a private room. He's about to open the door, but hesitates, narrowing his gaze on me. "What you said to the nurse before… Is it true?"

I stare at him for several protracted seconds, unsure what to say. Up until this point, I didn't want to think of Finn as the father of my child. This was supposed to be my baby.

But after seeing my father, after seeing what taking the easy way gets you, I don't want that anymore. I want people to know I'm carrying Finn's baby, regardless of whether he still wants me or not.

"It is."

Something flickers across Hayden's face before the corners of his mouth lift. A rare, genuine smile. Then he does something I don't expect. He wraps me in a hug.

"Congratulations," he murmurs.

I squeeze my eyes shut, emotion swelling in my chest.

When he pulls back, his hand settles on my shoulder. "I don't know what's going on between you two, but I do know this. Finn is one of the best people I know. And he'll be an amazing father."

"I know he will be."

He gives my shoulder a squeeze. "I'll give you some privacy."

I face the door once more, and take a deep breath before pushing it open.

It doesn't matter that Hayden told me what happened. Nothing could have prepared me for the sight of my best friend propped up in the hospital bed, his face streaked with soot, a bandage wrapped around his forearm. His leg is in a brace and bruises dot his arms.

But he's alive. He's here.

I didn't lose him without telling him how I really feel.

His head turns at the sound of the door, and when our eyes meet, something shifts in his expression. Almost like relief.

"Genevieve," he exhales, shifting like he wants to sit up straighter, but I'm at his side before he can try. "I'm so sorry." He reaches for my face, swiping away my tears. "I didn't mean to scare you."

I choke out a relieved sob. This is typical Finn. Always apologizing for things that aren't his fault. Always putting everyone else before himself.

It only solidifies what I've always known.

He's the only man for me.

"I thought I was doing what was right," I blurt out, my voice unsteady. "Keeping my distance. Pushing you away. I thought it was the safe thing. The easy thing. If I didn't let myself need you, if I didn't let myself love you, I couldn't lose you, but I was wrong."

"You were?"

I nod, not looking away from his eyes. "I wasn't protecting myself. I was hiding. I convinced myself that being alone was safer. That if I never let anyone too close, I'd never have to feel the kind of pain that rips you apart." I shake my head, exhaling sharply. "But that's exactly what I've felt since I let you go, Finn. This pain… It's the most excruciating thing I've ever experienced. I don't want to feel this way anymore. I don't want easy anymore. I want real. And what I feel for you…" My voice wavers. "It's the most real thing I've ever known."

His chest rises and falls, his fingers squeezing mine like they're the only thing keeping him tethered.

"And how do you——"

"I love you," I whisper before he can finish.

His whole body stills.

The seconds stretch between us, heavy and charged, until he finally breathes, "Genevieve…"

"I think I've loved you for years," I admit, the words tumbling out before I can stop them. "But I was too scared to admit it. Too scared to lose you. You've been my constant. My home. The one person who never gave up on me, even when I pushed you away. I don't want to be scared anymore. I don't want to waste another second convincing myself I don't need you, when the truth is, I need you like I need air."

His jaw clenches, his eyes flashing with something raw and unguarded.

"And I'm not just saying all of this because you could have died today. In fact, I was on my way to the station to tell you all of this when Murphy called me."

"You were?"

I nod. "I don't want to raise this baby alone. I want you in our child's life as his or her father. Not out of obligation. But because I want this with you, Finn. I want us."

His breath shudders out. "You want us?"

"More than anything."

For a moment, all I hear is the beeping of the monitors, the distant hum of hospital noise. Then he reaches for my face, his fingers threading into my hair, pulling me closer until our foreheads brush.

"Say it again," he murmurs, his voice barely above a whisper.

"I want us."

He shakes his head. "Not that."

I don't need to ask what he means.

"I love you," I breathe.

A quiet, almost broken sound leaves his throat.

"It's about damn time," he rasps.

Then his lips crash against mine.

It's not tentative. It's not careful.

It's years of longing. Of missed chances. Of words left unspoken.

It's an apology and a promise. A declaration and a vow.

I melt into him, my hands gripping his hospital gown, holding on like I never want to let go.

And I won't have to.

Because Finn has proven time and again he'll never give up on me. That he'll never abandon me.

And that's enough for me.

THIRTY-EIGHT

Finn

I shift my weight from foot to foot, a subtle ache in my leg even though the bone has finally healed, allowing me to return to work full time. For the first time since I left the army and joined the fire department, I considered walking away. Doing something safer. After all, I'm going to be a father.

But Genevieve wouldn't hear of it. She knows I always dreamed of being a firefighter, even as a little boy. Plus, she refused to spend the rest of her life with someone who complained about their job.

I didn't think it was possible to fall even more in love with her. But since she showed up at the hospital and finally admitted her feelings, I've learned anything's possible. And every day, I find another reason to love her even more.

The scent of roasted chestnuts and spiced cider surrounds me, mingling with the sweet aroma of pine drifting from the towering Norway spruce as I make my way through the crowds at Holley Ridge's annual Christmas Festival.

A few months ago, I wouldn't have given this scene much thought. Now, though? Now I can't stop watching her.

Genevieve stands by the ice skating rink talking to Dylan, her laughter rising above the sounds of holiday music and the occasional scrape of skate blades against ice. Twinkling Christmas lights reflect in her eyes, making them shine even brighter, and the cold has left her cheeks pink, her breath curling in soft clouds with every exhale.

It's not just the holiday glow that has me mesmerized.

It's the way her hand drifts absentmindedly to her belly, cradling the small curve beneath her wool coat, a silent reminder that, in a matter of months, the girl who's been my best friend my entire life will give birth to our daughter.

Our daughter.

Since finding out the gender a few weeks ago, I've spent a ridiculous amount of money on baby clothes, much to Genevieve's dismay. She keeps telling me the baby will practically live in onesies and pajamas for the first few months, but I can't help myself. Every tiny dress, every pair of ruffled socks… I want them all. It's a strange feeling, considering not that long ago, I was perfectly content living the single life.

Finding that damn list of sperm donors changed everything. And I couldn't be happier.

"You are a lifesaver," Genevieve says when I approach, her eyes focused on the two steaming cups in my hands. "I've been craving hot chocolate since we got here."

"Anything for you." I give her one, my fingers brushing against hers for a second longer than necessary.

"Where's mine?" Dylan asks as I'm about to take a sip.

"Do you really want one?"

She gives me a sly smile. "I'll grab one myself in a bit. Or maybe go steal some of Beckham's mulled wine."

"He says it's a good batch," I say, sipping on my drink.

As much as I enjoy the wine my brother makes, I decided to give up drinking during Genevieve's pregnancy.

Plus, she's unusually sensitive to the smell of alcohol. I came home after having one beer at Jude's brewery early on in the pregnancy and she made me sleep on the couch, the stench too strong for her.

After that, I decided it wasn't worth it. I'd much

rather share a bed with the woman I love than have a few drinks with friends.

A familiar squeal cuts through the air and I look at the rink. Presley and Jeremiah are bundled in puffy coats and skates, their hands gripping onto a woman I don't recognize.

She's young, early to mid-twenties, with dark hair spilling from beneath a knit beanie. Her soft laughter rings through the air as she guides Jeremiah across the ice, letting him cling to her arm as he wobbles and nearly face-plants, all while still keeping a close eye on Presley.

"Who's that?" I ask Dylan, my brows scrunched.

"Her name's Rowan," my sister responds casually. "She's the new nanny."

"What happened to the last one?"

She scoffs. "Hayden fired her."

"Didn't he fire the one before, too?"

"And the one before that. And the one before that. He tried to bribe me to come back, but I refused. Don't get me wrong," she adds quickly. "I love those kids, but I've been putting my own needs second for too long. Between working for Jude at the brewery and helping with Hayden's kids, I haven't pursued anything for myself. And that's going to change."

I tilt my head, studying the determined set of her jaw. "How so?"

Her eyes gleam with excitement. "Eden and I are

starting a personal chef service. There's a huge demand for it, especially being so close to Tahoe. I'm finally taking a risk and doing something for myself."

I grab her hand, squeezing it. "I'm happy for you."

"I'm sure you'll do great," Genevieve chimes in.

"It's scary, but if it's not scary, it's not worth it. Right?" I look down at Genevieve, and our eyes meet. A quiet understanding passes between us.

"The best things in life usually are," she murmurs, her voice softer now.

I start to lower my lips to hers, but the sound of a commotion cuts through.

I snap my attention back to the rink just in time to see Rowan lose her balance. She tries to catch herself, arms flailing, but her skates betray her, and she crashes onto the ice with a surprised yelp.

Hayden, who had been watching from the sidelines, moves before I fully process what's happening. One second, he's standing stiffly with his hands shoved into his coat pockets. The next, he's on the ice, crouched beside Rowan, his expression unreadable.

Almost…panicked.

"Hmm," Genevieve muses, a knowing smile curving her lips.

I frown. "What?"

"She has him so rattled," Dylan answers for her.

I watch as Hayden helps Rowan back to her feet,

but doesn't immediately let go. Instead, he seems to study every inch of her face.

Then he jumps back, almost losing his balance. He shakes his head and turns away, but Rowan watches him for a beat longer, like she's trying to figure him out.

"I'm going to grab some mulled wine," Dylan announces, pushing off the fence. "Do you need anything?" she asks Genevieve.

"I'm fine."

"Good." She squeezes her shoulder, then starts toward the rows of stalls filled with locals selling various holiday-themed items.

"What about me?" I call out after her. "You didn't ask me if I needed anything."

"You're not turning food into a human. Get it yourself." She playfully flips me the bird, and I feign indignation.

"There are children around, Dylan."

"That's why all I did was flip you off." She throws a wink my way before disappearing into the crowd.

I glance around, taking in the familiar scene — the towering spruce, the makeshift North Pole, the glow of soft lights reflecting off the lake.

I've come to the Holley Ridge Christmas Festival every year for as long as I can remember.

But this year?

This year feels different.

Because this will be the last year it'll be just Genevieve and me.

Next year, we'll have our daughter bundled in a tiny coat. Watching the lights with wide, curious eyes. Meeting Santa for the first time.

"Claire did a great job," I say, admiring the cozy wonderland around us. "The place looks like something out of a greeting card."

"She did. Didn't she?" Genevieve's voice softens with pride.

While Parker, the owner of Holley Ridge, typically planned every single detail of the annual Holley Ridge Holiday Festival, this year she handed off most of the planning to Claire as the new head of marketing, which allowed Parker to not work every waking hour of the day.

"She was definitely nervous, considering she has big shoes to fill. But she's a smart girl. Smarter than she gives herself credit for."

"Who's that with her?" I lift my cup for a sip, nodding toward the pair walking along the snow-dusted path beside the lake.

Claire's bundled in a red coat and knit hat, cheeks flushed from the cold. The man next to her is tall, all crisp lines and tailored edges. He walks like he owns whatever room, or snowy festival, he steps into.

"I've never seen him before."

Genevieve follows my line of sight. "That's Joshua's dad, Declan."

I arch a brow. "His dad?"

Over the years of my friendship with Genevieve, I've spent time with Claire's on-again, off-again boyfriend turned close friend, and know he grew up without a father much like Claire and Genevieve. But unlike with Claire and Genevieve, his father didn't intentionally abandon him. Instead, Joshua was the result of a one-night stand.

"Apparently he did one of those DNA ancestry things and got a notification he had a close familial match. His father. So he reached out and they agreed to meet."

I study the man again. Slate gray overcoat, leather gloves, the kind of man who probably has a personal tailor and regular massage appointments.

"So that's Joshua's dad?"

"That's what I said," Genevieve sings in response.

"Interesting."

She tilts her head, her brow furrowed. "What is?"

I lean closer so no one can overhear. "Because he's not looking at Claire like she's his son's ex-girlfriend."

"What are you talking about?"

"And she's not looking at him like he's her ex-boyfriend's dad."

"From the guy who couldn't see his own brother eye-fucking the new nanny." She rolls her eyes as she brings her cup to her lips. "There's nothing going on between Claire and Declan."

"Trust me on this." I take a satisfied sip of my hot cocoa.

She opens her mouth, ready to fire back, then pauses. Her gaze drifts toward Claire and Declan again, and I know she sees it now. The extra beat their eyes hold. The way Claire's laughter is a touch too breathless. How Declan stands just a little too close, like he doesn't even realize he's doing it.

"He…" Genevieve trails off.

"What?" I nudge. "Finally realizing I'm right?"

"No, I just…" She shifts beside me, placing a hand on her stomach. "Oh, wow."

I straighten immediately, my heart thudding, all thoughts of Claire and Joshua's father disappearing. "What is it? Are you okay?"

She exhales, adjusting again, then grabs my gloved hand and presses it to her stomach. "Hold it there."

At first, I feel nothing.

Then a small, but insistent nudge pokes against my palm. A tiny, deliberate kick, like a secret message from the life we created.

"That's… That's her?" My voice is rough, barely a whisper.

She nods, her eyes shining. "That's her."

A slow exhale leaves me. I've seen her during an ultrasound, watched the flickering heartbeat, but this?

This is real in a way I wasn't prepared for. A living, breathing piece of us. Of the love we share.

I slip off my glove, desperate to feel her without layers between us.

And our little girl delivers.

"That's…incredible." I press my forehead to hers, my voice thick. "You're incredible. I love you so damn much, Genevieve. You and little bean. Our little family."

She sighs into me. "Our little family."

THIRTY-NINE

Genevieve

The barn at Holley Ridge is warm with candlelight, golden flickers dancing against the exposed wood beams. Twinkle lights drape overhead like stars, casting everything in a soft, dreamlike glow. The scent of fresh roses and aged wood fills the air, blending with the faint aroma of the crisp autumn night drifting through the open doors.

"Tell me I'm not going to cry."

Claire laughs, adjusting the delicate lace material of my dress, her fingers steady where mine are shaking.

"Oh, you are absolutely going to cry."

She's right. My heart is already too full.

I glance at my mom standing on the other side of me, my daughter nestled in her arms. She's swaddled in a blanket Finn's mom knitted, her round cheeks pink. She lets out a soft coo, and I lean down, touching a tender kiss to her forehead.

Four months ago, I held this little girl for the first time, overwhelmed by a love I never knew existed. Now, I can't imagine a world without little Sophia in it. She's the life I created with my best friend. A tangible piece of our story, nestled in my mother's arms, watching with curious eyes as if she somehow understands the weight of this moment.

Claire gives my arm a gentle squeeze, pulling my attention away from my daughter. "Ready?"

I give her a bright smile. "More than ready."

"Good."

She turns her attention to one of the event planners, letting them know to start the processional. I give one last kiss to Sophia before Claire, Dylan, and my mother line up, each disappearing in turn.

Then the music changes, and I step forward, appearing at the end of the aisle. All the guests shift their attention to me, but I don't see any of them.

I only see Finn.

My best friend.

The father of my child.

The man who's loved me his entire life.

Finn's brothers stand beside him, a wall of familiar faces, all wearing matching grins.

But it's Finn I can't look away from.

His blue eyes hold me captive, bright with something I've never seen in them before. Not just love, but certainty. As if this moment was always inevitable.

My feet carry me forward until I reach him. He takes my hands in his, steady and warm, grounding me in a way only he can.

"Hi, baby." His voice is hushed, familiar, like a whispered promise in the dark.

I let out a soft, breathless laugh. "Hi."

"You two ready?" Grandma Estelle asks with a raised brow.

We both nod eagerly.

"Thought so." She winks, then addresses our closest friends and family. "Ladies and gentlemen, I'm honored to be here today to celebrate the long-awaited union of Finnegan Evan Lawrence to Genevieve Patricia Thomas.

"Now, I've read a lot of romance novels in my time on this planet. Some sweet. Some steamy. And some that would make a grown man blush."

Everyone erupts in laughter, myself included.

"And let me tell you, this right here? This is the kind of love story I live for. Small-town boy loves small-town girl for years, pines for her in tortured silence, probably does a lot of brooding, and then offers to knock her up. That's what we call a plot twist, folks."

I smile at Finn, a warmth spreading through me at the reminder of how we ended up here. What would have happened if he never discovered my list? If he never offered to help me have a baby? Would we have eventually found our way to each other? Or would we have gone through life fighting our feelings?

Thankfully, I'll never have to find out.

"I've seen you moon over Genevieve since she was knee-high to a grasshopper," Grandma Estelle continues. "Honestly, it's about time you put a ring on it. We were all getting a little impatient. Some of us had bets on whether you'd get there before your AARP card arrived."

Another burst of laughter echoes through the high ceilings of the barn. Then Grandma Estelle turns her attention on me. "And Genevieve, sweetheart, you're marrying a firefighter. A man who can literally carry you out of danger and make you breakfast after. If that's not the dream, I don't know what is. Your own book boyfriend in real life."

"He definitely is," I agree.

"But enough of my rambling. We're here to make this thing legal before one of you changes your mind. Though, let's be honest, Finn would rather run into a burning building than let this woman get away again."

"Damn straight," he remarks with a smirk.

"Then let's get you two married."

Grandma Estelle shifts gears, talking about the importance of friendship in marriage, but the words barely register. All I can focus on is Finn. The way he watches me like he's still memorizing every inch of my face. The way his thumb strokes soft circles over my knuckles, like he knows I need the reassurance.

Then Grandma Estelle announces it's time for the vows, giving me the go ahead to begin.

I swallow, my pulse racing. "I wrote these months ago. And then I rewrote them. And then I rewrote them again. Because how do you put into words what you mean to me?" I choke out, overwhelmed with emotion.

Finn's grip tightens slightly, a silent encouragement, and I take a breath.

"For most of my life, I believed love was something that never stayed. I thought if I never needed it, I'd never lose it. I told myself I was better off alone than risking heartbreak again. But then there was you," I whisper. "There was always you."

His jaw clenches, his throat working against emotion.

"The person who saw me when I felt invisible. The man who stood beside me long before I was ready to stand beside him. I spent years running from the love you offered so freely. And when I finally stopped running, when I let myself love you back, I realized something." My lashes dampen with tears. "Sometimes you need to get lost to find yourself. And I found myself in you. In your unwavering devotion. In your unyielding love."

I take a steadying breath to try to collect myself. Then I continue.

"I promise to love you for all the years I should have loved you sooner. I promise to choose you every day. To let you carry the hard things with me, even when I think I have to carry them alone." My lips tremble. "For as long as I can remember, you've been my best friend. My safe place. My home. And I promise I'll never take that for granted again."

Finn's eyes shine with unshed tears, his fingers brushing my knuckles in silent understanding.

Then a soft sound breaks the moment.

Sophia lets out a tiny, gurgling giggle, her little hand flailing in the air.

Finn chuckles, stepping forward before anyone can stop him, and takes her from my mom's arms, cradling her against his chest.

The sight does something to me.

Big, broad Finn Lawrence in his casual suit holding something so small and precious. His hand, impossibly gentle as he smooths a knuckle over her soft cheek.

"She wanted to be part of this," he murmurs, briefly lifting his gaze to mine before returning it to our daughter. He leans down and presses a kiss to her soft skin. "You always know when to steal the show, don't you, baby girl?"

A ripple of laughter moves through our guests, but my heart is no longer in my chest. It's in Finn's arms. Beating right there with him and the little life we created.

Finn gives her back to my mom, then returns to me, slipping a hand into his pocket. I expect him to pull out notecards containing his vows. But that's not the case.

My eyes widen as I stare at the familiar paper.

At the list Claire and I made that night at Jude's brewery, when I thought I could plan my future with logic instead of love.

"I, uh, found something a few weeks ago," Finn begins, unfolding the paper with slow precision. "I thought about making my own list. A list of all the reasons I've loved you since we were kids. But we agreed to keep our vows short."

He flashes me a smile as laughter murmurs through the barn. Then he shifts his eyes to the paper.

"You wrote that the father of your child should be healthy." He returns his gaze to mine. "I promise to take care of myself so I can always be there for you. For our daughter. So I can spend as much time with the most important people to me."

Tears prick my eyes, my throat tight with emotion.

His Adam's apple bobs up and down as he looks at the paper once more. "You said he should be intelligent." A soft chuckle rumbles from his throat. "I can't promise I'll always be the smartest guy in the room, but I will never stop learning how to love you better. Never stop learning how to be a better husband. Never stop learning how to be the best father our daughter can ask for."

I pull my lips between my teeth to stop my chin from quivering, but it's a losing battle.

"You wrote that he should be kind. That he should be compassionate. That he should be gentle. I hope I'm all of those things. I hope I always will be."

"You are," I tell him.

"But as much as I want to say you covered all the bases with this…" He holds up the piece of paper before tucking it back into his pocket. "My original assessment still stands. You left something important off this list."

"What's that?"

Finn steps closer and takes my hands in his once more.

"Love, Genevieve." His thumb skims my skin. "You forgot love. I think we both know that's the part that matters most."

His eyes lock onto mine with an intensity that steals the air from my lungs.

"I promise to love you in every way I know how," he murmurs, his voice thick, reverent. "To remind you every single day that you are my best friend, my love, my family.

"I promise to be the man who never lets you face your troubles alone. To be the arms you run to when life feels too heavy. And the hand you hold when you realize you don't have to run at all."

A tear slips down my cheek, and Finn lifts one of our joined hands, brushing his lips over my knuckles.

"I promise to never let you forget how much you are loved, even in the moments you try to convince yourself otherwise.

"I promise to stand beside you when things are easy, and to fight for you when they aren't. I promise to be the kind of man our daughter can look at and know without a single shred of doubt what love is supposed to look like."

I let out a shaky breath, and Finn tightens his hold on my hands. "I spent years thinking you'd never be mine. And now that you are, I promise…" His voice wavers, his eyes glistening. "I promise to spend the rest of my life making sure you never regret choosing me. You are my beginning, my middle, and my ever after."

"And you're mine," I manage to whisper.

Grandma Estelle says something about rings, but I barely register it through the thick haze of emotion. I only know Finn's hands are steady as he slides the band onto my finger. That when he kisses me, the barn erupts in cheers.

And that when he finally pulls back, his love shining in his eyes, this isn't just what I wanted.

It's what I was always meant to have.

Thank you so much for reading *Friends with Baby Benefits*.

Wondering about Hayden and the nanny? Find out today in Tempted by the Nanny!

She's my employee. Off-limits. And more than ten years younger than me. Yet, I can't stop wanting her.

In the mood for a spicy holiday romance? Then check out Claire's story in *The One Night Stand Before Christmas*!

The only thing worse than having a one-night stand with a ridiculously hot stranger during a snowstorm in Boston? Finding out he's your ex-boyfriend's father.

Want one last taste of Finn and Genevieve? Then sign up for my mailing list to get a bonus chapter. Just enter the link into a web browser or scan the code below.

https://geni.us/BabyBonusTL

Thank you so much for taking the time to read this book. If you enjoyed it, please let your friends know by leaving a review so more people can fall in love with Finn and Genevieve.

TEMPTED
by the
NANNY

I'm the nanny for a grumpy single dad.
And the heart keeping me alive?
It belonged to his late wife.

Working as a nanny for Dr. Hayden Lawrence was supposed to be simple. Keep my head down, take care of his adorable kids, and absolutely do not notice the way his rolled-up sleeves make me weak in the knees.

I'm sunshine.
He's a grumpy doctor.

I believe in saying yes to things that scare me.
He believes in control, order, and never loving again.

We are complete opposites.

But living together has a way of blurring lines.

Late-night talks in the kitchen.

Lingering touches when he hands me the baby.

The way his daughter wraps her arms around my waist like I already belong.

Falling for him was never part of the plan.

Neither was learning the heart beating inside my chest once belonged to his late wife.

If I tell him my second chance at life began with his worst nightmare, it could shatter the fragile peace he's fought so hard to rebuild.

I'm not sure which is more terrifying… Losing him, or asking him to gamble his heart on a future that's anything but certain.

The *one* NIGHT *stand* *before* CHRISTMAS

The only thing worse than having a one-night stand with a ridiculously hot stranger during a snowstorm in Boston?

Finding out he's your ex-boyfriend's father.

In my defense, I didn't know the tall, broody man in the tailored suit would turn out to be Joshua's dad.

I also didn't expect him to spend Christmas in my quaint small town of Sycamore Falls.

Or attend every single one of the town's holiday events.

Or look at me like we're still back in that hotel room.

Now I'm currently one awkward sleigh ride away from a full-blown holiday meltdown. Because Declan Hart? He has bad idea written all over him.

Not only is he some hotshot attorney with a military past, but he has a voice as smooth as whiskey and a body that makes my tinsel curl.

He's also completely off-limits.

Which wouldn't be a problem…

If I could just stop thinking about that night.

Or how his eyes light up in the snow.

Or what might happen if we get caught under the mistletoe again.

This Christmas, I might be the one getting tangled up in something I really shouldn't want.

The One Night Stand Before Christmas is a small town, forbidden age gap holiday romance. Grab your copy today!

ACKNOWLEDGMENTS

Thank you so much for reading *Friends with Baby Benefits*. I hope you enjoyed reading Finn and Genevieve's story! These days it seems everyone wants an angst-filled enemies-to-lovers story, but I will always love a heartwarming friends-to-lovers story. There's just something about two lifetime best friends finally realizing what everyone's been trying to tell them for years. I just hope I didn't make it too angsty for you!

Before I start working on my next book, I wanted to take a minute to thank all of the people who help behind the scenes.

First of all, a big thank you to my family — Stan and Harper Leigh. Thanks for your unwavering support over the years.

To my wonderful PA, Melissa Crump — thanks

for everything you do to keep me as organized as possible.

To my fantastic beta readers — Lin, Melissa, Stacy, Sylvia, and Vicky — thank you so much for taking the time to read my rough drafts and offer feedback. It means the world to me.

To my admin team — Melissa and Vicky. Thank you for keeping me sane and keeping my social media running so I can write.

To my review team — Thanks for reading and reviewing my books. With all the books out there, I'm grateful you've found and enjoyed mine enough to want to join my team.

To my reader group — Thanks for being my super-fans and giving me a place to go when I need a break from writing.

And last but not least, a big thank you to YOU! Thank you so much for picking up this book and taking a chance on it. Whether you've been a long-time T.K. Leigh reader or are just finding me now in this new genre, I'm so happy you took the time to read my words.

Until next time…

Love & Peace,
  ~ T.K.

ABOUT *the* AUTHOR

Tracy Leigh is the spicy small town alter ego of USA Today Bestselling author T.K. Leigh. She lives outside of Raleigh with her husband, daughter, special needs rescue dog, and three cats.

When she's not penning her next small town romance filled with heat and heart, she can be found reading, spending time with her family, or planning her next escape to Hawaii.

facebook.com/tracyleighbooks

instagram.com/tkleigh

tiktok.com/@tracyleighauthor

bookbub.com/authors/t-k-leigh

pinterest.com/tkleighauthor